THERE ARE JEWS IN MY HOUSE

THERE ARE JEWS IN MY HOUSE

LARA VAPNYAR

Pantheon Books, New York

Special thanks to *Open City,* where both "Mistress"
and "There Are Jews in My House" were originally
published. Thanks also to *The New Yorker,*
which published "Love Lessons."

Library of Congress Cataloging-in-Publication Data
Vapnyar, Laura, 1971–
There are Jews in my house / Laura Vapnyar.
p. cm.
ISBN 0-375-42250-1
1. United States—Social life and customs—Fiction.
2. Russia—Social Life and customs—Fiction.
3. Jews—United States—Fiction.
4. Jews—Russia—Fiction. I. Title.
PS3622.A68T47 2003
813'.6—dc21   2003042975

www.pantheonbooks.com
Book design by Robert C. Olsson

Printed in the United States of America
First Edition
9 8 7 6 5 4 3 2 1

CONTENTS

THERE ARE JEWS IN MY HOUSE

There Are Jews in My House

GALINA CARRIED in an aluminum pot of boiled potatoes, holding it by the handles with a kitchen towel.
She put it on a wooden holder in the middle of a round
table covered with a beige oilcloth. She opened the lid and,
turning her face away from the steam, ladled coarse, unpeeled potatoes onto each of the four plates. The plates
were beautiful: delicate, white, with a golden rim and little
forget-me-nots in the center.

For the past six weeks, they'd been eating in the living
room, where the heavy dark brown curtains covered the
only window. For the past two weeks, they'd been eating in
silence. From time to time, somebody coughed or sneezed,
the girls might whisper something to each other, or even
giggle, after which they glanced guiltily at their mothers,
but mostly they heard only themselves blowing on their
food and the clatter of heavy silver forks. Galina didn't
mind the silence. It was better than having to talk, to keep

up a forced conversation, as she did a few weeks before. Even the room itself was best suited for silence. It was large and square, empty and spotless. The sparse furniture was drawn close to the walls, and there was only a massive dinner table in the middle, rising like an island on the dark brown floorboards.

Since they dined on potatoes everyday, Galina was used to everybody's eating habits. Her seven-year-old daughter, Tanya, cut the potato in half and bit the insides out of the skin hurriedly, then ate the skins too. Raya, sitting across from Galina, peeled potatoes for herself and her eight-year-old daughter, Leeza. "Two princesses," Galina thought. Raya peeled potatoes with her hands, using her delicate fingernails to hook the skins. She bent her head so low that her dingy hair almost touched her plate. Raya and Leeza broke their peeled potatoes into small pieces and ate, picking them up with a fork. Raya's hands were often shaking, and then the fork clutched in her fingers was shaking too, knocking on the plate with an unnerving tinkling sound. Galina had the urge to catch that trembling fork and hold it tight, not to let it shake. "Chew, chew!" Galina kept saying to Tanya, who tended to swallow big chunks in a hungry rush. "You're wasting your food when you're not chewing." Galina herself ate slowly. She picked up a whole potato on a fork and ate it with the skin, biting off pieces with her strong, wide teeth. She chewed zealously, careful not to waste food and also trying to prolong dinner as much as possible, because the hours between dinner and going to bed were the most unbearable.

Six weeks ago, when Raya and Leeza first came to live at Galina's place, it had been different. Galina and Raya spent the evenings talking, mostly about the prewar life that seemed now unreal and perfect. They retold some minor episodes in meticulous detail, as if the precision of their memories could turn that prewar life into something real, and failure to remember something could unlock the door of Galina's apartment and let the war in. If one of them was unsure of a detail, she relied on the memory of the other. "I used to buy Moscow rolls every Saturday. Remember, Moscow rolls, the small ones with the striped crust? They were six kopecks each. Were they six kopecks?" "I think they were seven—the ones with poppy seeds cost six." Often, their conversations went on well into the night, after the girls had fallen asleep. Then they moved closer to each other and talked in whispers.

Now, right after dinner, Raya went into the back room, where she and Leeza slept, and sat there on the bed with her back to Galina. Sometimes, Raya bent over the nightstand and started a letter—to her husband no doubt—but after a few lines she always stopped and crumpled the paper. At other times, Raya had a book in her hands, but she didn't turn the pages. Through the opened door—Raya never shut the door—Galina saw Raya's pale, unclean neck, so thin that you could count every vertebra. Galina couldn't concentrate on a book either. She would follow the lines to the bottom of the page and only then realize that the letters didn't form words and sentences, but simply passed in front of her eyes like endless rows of black beads.

5

Galina dried the dishes and stacked them in the cupboard above her head. She put the aluminum pot on the lower shelf, shoving it deeper with her foot, then shut the cupboard door with a bang. She wondered if Raya heard the clatter. Sharp sounds made Raya shudder. Everything. A fork falling on the floor, a door's squeak, somebody's sneezing, the toilet flushing. For a long time, Galina had tried to do everything as quietly as possible. Now she didn't care. Raya herself was quiet as a mouse. That's what she told Galina when she came: "I'll be quiet as a mouse." Galina wondered then where this expression came from, why mice were considered so quiet. Because they weren't. Galina grew up in the country, and there were a lot of mice in their house. At night, they made these distinctive mice sounds—scratching and nibbling and knocking against the floor with their tiny claws when they ran from one corner to another. Little Galina lay in bed thinking that if she opened her eyes she would see a mouse with crooked yellow teeth and moist eyes staring right at her.

Galina went into the living room, removing her wet apron. The usual picture: the girls were on the sofa, making a dress for Leeza's doll from some scraps. As always, Tanya was doing all the work and Leeza giving instructions, Galina thought with annoyance. The doll's pink, shiny body was turning swiftly in Tanya's hands as she dressed her. It was a beautiful, expensive doll with the torso made from hard plastic and the head and limbs from some other, softer kind. It had blond hair shaped into long, springy curls and round light blue eyes that seemed to stare right at you. Galina didn't have toys like that as a child, and she couldn't afford to buy them for Tanya.

Galina peeked into the back room. Raya didn't turn to her, only bent lower. She was scribbling something with Galina's rusty ink pen. The pen was almost dry and made heart-rending sounds, scratching the paper.

Galina covered her ears and looked around. She had always liked that her room was so plain. There weren't any crocheted doilies, marble elephants, or crystal vases. The windowsills weren't decorated with pots of geraniums, the floors with rugs, or the walls with framed paintings. She didn't even have an image of the Madonna in the corner where it always hung in her mother's house. The only thing on the wall was a framed black-and-white photograph of Galina's mother. Now, Galina wished they had a painting— any painting, something to rest her gaze on. She uncovered her ears and immediately heard the awful scratching sound of Raya's pen, Leeza's troubled breathing, the snapping of the big tailor's scissors in Tanya's hands, Leeza's cackling cough. Galina wanted to scream, open her mouth and scream at the top of her lungs.

She rushed to the hall, mumbling that she was going to get some air before the curfew. She wondered if Raya heard her. She probably didn't. Because if she did, she would have darted out of the back room, asking: "What? What did you just say? You're going where?" Her face would have been distorted and her voice faltering. During the last few days, it happened every time Galina went out of the house. Every time. When Galina went to the market in the morning,

7

when she left to talk with one of the neighbors or their former coworkers, when she simply went out for a breath of fresh air, like today. Every time, when Galina touched the doorknob of the exit door, she felt Raya's begging stare on her. She saw that Raya wanted to fall on her knees, to clutch at the edge of Galina's dress and not let her go. But she didn't do it, she just stood in the doorway, shifting from one foot to the other, clasping the doorframe with yellowed fingers, clearing her throat to ask in her thin, trembling voice again and again: "Where're you going? When will you be back?"

Galina opened the door and glanced in the direction of the back room. Raya hadn't moved.

Galina walked downstairs, trying to resist an urge to run. Part of her was expecting Raya to rush out the door and grab her by the sleeve. A ridiculous thought. Galina knew that Raya would never so much as stick her head out. She walked to the door and pushed the cold iron handle down. The door gave in slowly, scratching the stone floor and making a tired screech, the last sound before the silence of the outside.

It was beginning to get dark, but still the contrast between the soft, dusky light of the street and the semidarkness of the staircase was great. Galina had to shield her eyes for a moment. Their deserted street with a few pale stone buildings, a few leafless trees, and broad rough sidewalks, was wide and airy. Galina threw her head back and inhaled hungrily. At last, she could breathe!

. . .

THE DECLARATION OF WAR with Germany three months ago, in June, although completely unexpected, didn't shake Galina. Somehow she didn't see the war as a great tragedy, as a disaster rushing into their lives and destroying everything. For her, it was more like an unwelcome change in her daily life, requiring some practical adjustments. Galina made her husband, Sergey, dig a big hole in the empty plot of land behind their building and construct a little cellar there, while she was buying potatoes, drying them in sheets of newspapers, and storing them in big sacks. Galina also bought large quantities of salt, soap, oil, and matches; glued stripes of paper to the windows to protect them from shells; made sure that she and Tanya had enough warm clothes; and determined the shortest route to the air-raid shelter, counting the number of steps. She didn't feel shaken—on the contrary, she felt energetic and alive, something that hadn't happened to her in a very long time. She also felt proud of being able to keep calm and make rational decisions at the time, while everybody else seemed to lose his head. Galina didn't feel shaken even when she saw her husband off to the front. They were stuck in the middle of the crowd of men going to the front and the howling children and women who were clutching the men's coats. Sergey was silent. The only words he said were about Tanya, that it was good that Galina didn't let her come along, that it would have been too upsetting. Galina thought it was good too. She saw a glimpse of Raya nearby, howling like the others, with her hands tightly locked on her husband's back. "Don't they understand?" Galina thought, starting to feel annoyed. "It's war, men are supposed to go."

Toward the end of the summer, when there was a clear prospect of the town being occupied, the evacuation started. The factory equipment was packed hastily in plywood boxes and put on freight trains along with valuable workers and the families of those soldiers who were members of the Communist Party. All the others (families of non-Communist soldiers, retired workers, and invalids) were supposed to follow in a few days. But in a few days, the town was cut off. Galina and Raya stayed, because neither of their husbands was a Communist.

The prospect of staying in the occupied town seemed uncomfortable to Galina, but not catastrophic, especially since Soviet newspapers said that the Germans treated the civilian population with decency. She had read it just a few weeks before the war. Galina made more practical adjustments: she buried all her modest valuables in the ground next to the potato sacks, she bought more soap and matches, she got rid of Tanya's red tie and a folder full of newspaper clippings about Stalin. Galina managed to keep her calm.

Raya was another matter. As soon as it was announced that the town would be cut off, she went into a feverish, panicky state. She spent the whole first day running around the station, grasping at anyone who would talk to her, begging the railroad officials to take her and Leeza on a freight train, trying to convince them that trains must run, simply because she, Raya, must leave. She continued to do that until she was forced away from the station along with the crowd of other desperate people. But, unlike them, Raya didn't give up after that. The following days she spent running around the town, attempting unthinkable measures to get her and Leeza out of town. She tried to bribe some truck drivers to drive them east. She tried to bribe a clerk in the city passport office to forge documents for them. She walked to the small villages to the south of town and asked everybody there if they could take her and Leeza out on horseback. When she came home from her day trips, the soles of her shoes were worn through and her feet rubbed raw. She slumped onto a couch and burst into hysterical sobs, unable to calm herself even in front of Leeza. Raya was Jewish. That explained a lot of things, Galina thought.

The war had been going on for a few months, and rumors became the only source of more or less credible information. The rumors about Jews differed. Some said that when Germans occupied a new town, the first thing they did was to put all the Jews on cattle trains and ship them away. Others said that Germans didn't bother to ship Jews anywhere; they just drove them together to the edge of a town or to a big ravine and shot them all. Everyone: men, women, and children. A few refugees from Kiev, where Raya's parents lived, added more ghastly details. Tanya began asking Galina: "Do they make Jews take off all their clothes? Underpants too? Do they throw all the Jews into a big pit and then burn them alive? Have they burned Leeza's grandma?" Galina told her to stop listening to nonsense. But Tanya wouldn't stop: "Do they also burn kids? Will they burn Leeza?" Galina told her to shut up. Raya also couldn't stop talking about that. She was running around town, looking for refugees and asking them more and more questions. She said she was sure that they were telling the truth. She said she could feel that her mother was dead.

It was hard to imagine Raya's mother dead. Galina had met her once or twice when she came to visit Raya. She was a very vivacious old woman—too vivacious in Galina's opinion. She wore silly hats and painted her lips, even though her face looked so obviously old, all wrinkled and puffy. She laughed a lot, showing her gold caps, and kissed Leeza in public. Galina tried to imagine Raya's mother as part of a gray, screaming crowd. She tried to imagine her naked, trying to cover her fat, wrinkled body, her silly hat still on. Did the hat fall off her head when they shot her, or did it stay, and Raya's mother's dead body was lying in a pit still attached to the hat?

It was Galina who found a solution for Raya. A peasant from a nearby village, a relative of Sergey, agreed to take Raya and Leeza in his wagon as far as the next town toward the eastern border. On the night they were supposed to leave, Galina came to see Raya off. Only then, seeing Raya and Leeza both dressed in their winter coats through it was a warm Indian summer night, seeing Raya's bursting-at-the-seams suitcase and Leeza's doll sticking out of her backpack, seeing their sturdy shoes and their grave faces, did Galina understand how real it was. Raya was leaving, leaving their town and leaving Galina all alone. Galina had an urge to grab Raya's hand and hold it, squeezing it harder and harder. She actually made a step toward Raya, but instead of taking her hand, Galina took the suitcase and carried it downstairs, clutching its cold leather handle.

THE ROAD LED Galina to the deserted tramlines. German officers and soldiers—there were only a few of them in their town—occupied brick buildings in the center, close to the City Hall. Here, in this remote part of town, the reality of the war wasn't so evident. There wasn't a grocery store or a movie theater nearby, and the area had always been deserted at that hour, after people had returned home from work.

It was very quiet. Galina had always associated war with noise: the swishing of missiles, explosions, the rumble of passing artillery, screams. But now it seemed that the outside world had been silenced around her. There were more disturbing signs of war inside Galina's apartment: the unplugged radio, the unpeeled potatoes, the traces of white paper on the windows, Raya's wary eyes, Raya's shaking hands, the sound of Raya's pen, the whole of Raya's being. Galina would never have imagined that it could be so hard to stand her presence.

. . .

GALINA AND RAYA met three years earlier, when Raya had moved into the town with her family and gotten a job as a junior librarian in the central library. It was the same position that Galina held. They sat at adjacent desks, went to lunch at the same little café on the corner, shopped in the same grocery store, and took the same tram to get home. They couldn't help but become friends. At the beginning, their main topic of conversation was the similarities in their lives. They loved to find more and more of them and then laugh in amazement. They lived on the same street in identical two-room apartments. They had daughters of almost the same age. Their husbands worked as engineers in the town's big textile factory. They were both outsiders in this town, having moved here because of their husbands' jobs. Neither had relatives or friends here. Raya had lived all her life in Kiev; Galina was born in a small village, but she went to school in Moscow and later lived there. So they were both used to life in big cities and found the town and their neighbors and coworkers very dull. They both were born in the beginning of March. They even looked alike: pretty, slender women of medium height, with blue eyes and wavy blond hair. Library customers often asked if they were sisters, making Raya shake with laughter and say that she had always wanted to have a sister. Once Raya talked Galina into buying identical dresses. They put them on in the Central Clothing Store's dressing room, and stood staring at each other in the large mirror. "We are twins!" Raya cried.

Another similarity was that they both passionately loved novels and often read them during working hours, causing puzzled looks from other library employees, who used working hours for knitting and chatting. Their favorite novel was *Anna Karenina* and, unlike everybody else, neither of them found the ending depressing. Raya said that for her the saddest part was the scene where Anna talked to her little son for the last time. "I cried for three hours straight," she said. "I would stop for a few minutes and then cry and cry again. My mother became panicky and wanted to run for the doctor," she added, laughing. "After that scene the rest of the novel simply couldn't touch me." Galina didn't cry when she read that scene or Anna's suicide scene. Galina felt paralyzed for days—paralyzed with envy for Anna Karenina. Anna could live a normal, stable life, but she chose not to. She opened the door and found a new, different life, where everything, even her suffering and death, was better than in her old life. Galina could almost visualize Anna opening the door—it was a heavy, rusty door, and Anna was pushing on it with her round shoulder. In Galina's life, there were no doors. Galina wondered if Raya could understand that.

Raya seemed to understand a lot of things. She understood when Galina told her about Sergey's drinking. Everybody else refused to understand how his drinking was a problem. "Does he beat you?" Other women asked, "Does he beat your daughter?" "Does he smash furniture and throw vases out of the window?" "Has he ever been found sleeping in a ditch?" No, Sergey had never done any of that. He was a quiet drunk—he came home every night, walked to his bed, shaking and staggering, and slumped down. The next morning, he woke up with a headache, and then he had an empty, dead expression in his eyes the whole day. He was also a shy, guilty drunk. When Galina asked where the money was that she had saved for Tanya's winter coat, his lips quivered and he turned away and swore in a trembling voice that it would never happen again. Other women didn't understand, maybe because their own husbands also drank and they weren't as shy and guilty as Sergey about it. Raya understood. She sat next to Galina and let her talk and cry, never interrupting her, never suggesting anything, only patting Galina's back from time to time and smiling at her softly. Raya also understood things that Galina had always considered private, her own, hidden from everybody else, nonexistent for other people. There often were sparks of recognition, when Raya described feelings and thoughts that Galina also secretly had. That pleased Galina—she wasn't alone. But at the same time, it frightened and appalled her—she didn't want to be faced with the reflection of herself in Raya. Once Raya said that she didn't love her husband. "I mean I love him very much," she corrected herself hurriedly. "But I don't . . . really love him." "I often have this uneasy feeling when I am around Leeza," Raya said another time. "Often I see that she is forcing herself to talk to me. She's never like that with her father. Sometimes,

I wonder if she loves me." Galina had wondered if her daughter loved her too. She seemed to be so much closer to her father. When Sergey was sober, they spent time making model airplanes, or playing chess or talking, bursting with laughter from time to time, but when Galina entered the room, their laughter always stopped abruptly. Galina tried to do things with Tanya too, but something always went wrong—Tanya became restless in a few minutes and Galina annoyed. "Do you love your daughter?" Galina wanted to ask Raya, but she didn't. She was afraid to hear the answer.

They didn't always talk about serious matters. Often they got together to chat about their lives, to share family anecdotes, stories about their adolescent crushes, cooking recipes, and makeup secrets. Or rather it was Raya who shared her makeup secrets, because Galina didn't know much about that kind of thing. Raya also knew a lot of tricks about underwear: "Galina, darling, don't stuff the whole thing in, bras are not for hiding your breasts—they are for pushing them up"; or about feminine hygiene: "You see, this way it will never leak, it will never stain your skirt again." Galina's fascination at these remarks was mixed with embarrassment—she'd never had anybody talk to her that way before.

They began spending more and more time together. Raya would drop by on weekends or after work, before her husband came home. Sometimes she brought Leeza and left her to play with Tanya in the living room while she and Galina talked in the kitchen. Galina often had things to do, and Raya sat at the kitchen table with a teacup in her hands.

Galina was moving about, wiping counters, scrubbing floors, cleaning carrots covered with layers of dirt, chopping gray chicken carcasses, or frying potatoes in a hissing skillet. When Sergey came home drunk, Galina got Tanya and they went to Raya's place to spend the evening. There they sat in Raya's messy kitchen and talked, often for hours. Raya never seemed to worry about cooking or cleaning. Galina thought that nothing, not even fire or flood, could distract Raya from talking. Once, Raya had a pot of soup boiling away on the stove. The white froth was pushing from under the lid, Raya saw it, but she didn't go to turn off the gas until she had finished her sentence. While they talked at Raya's place, the girls were usually playing in the back room, and Misha, Raya's husband, was lying on the living room couch with a book. Sometimes, Misha came out into the kitchen and asked apologetically if there was something to eat. Raya would jump off her chair and say that she was sorry and that she had forgotten all about dinner. She then began running around the kitchen trying to fix a meal—something very different from what was served in Galina's house. Dishes clattered, packages fell out of cupboards, and pieces of food dropped onto the floor. Sometimes, Galina stayed to help, and they cooked a meal together and then ate dinner together—all five of them.

THE SIDEWALK WAS SCATTERED with piles of slimy autumn leaves. They gave out a strange, sweetish smell when Galina touched them with her foot. Her toes were slowly getting chilly. Galina stepped over the glistening tram rails and started walking between the wooden ties. The dry gravel rustled under the thin soles of her boots. She had a pleasant prickly sensation in her feet every time she stepped on a little pebble. She didn't know where she was walking, just away from home, away from Raya.

GALINA HAD NEVER LIKED their dinners at Raya's place. She sensed that Raya and Misha were tense, tense and maybe a little embarrassed, because they had cheese and salami and canned sardines and early tomatoes on their table—things that Galina couldn't afford. Galina felt uncomfortable. Tanya's behavior made her feel even worse. She grabbed slices of salami from the plate—several slices at once—and said with her mouth full that she never thought "sausage" could be so delicious. She stuffed quartered tomatoes into her mouth, spurting red juice along with the seeds, and smiled happily. All of that in contrast with Leeza, who ate slowly, reluctantly, after being begged by Raya: "Darling, please, one more piece." Galina often felt the urge to smack Tanya on the back of her head, smack her hard, so that damned slice of salami would fall out of her mouth.

Misha's presence also made Galina uncomfortable. She avoided looking at him, probably because he was so unattractive, even ugly. Galina remembered now how stricken she was when she saw Misha for the first time. Raya and Leeza had come over for Sergey's birthday, but Misha was late. When he came in, the apartment was already packed with people. He entered timidly, towering above the sea of heads and clouds of tobacco smoke. He searched the room with his eyes, looking lost, and Galina for a second thought that he'd come there by mistake, he looked so different from everybody else. Misha had a small torso and a small head and very long, clumsy limbs. His neck was also very long, his nose large and wide. Raya called him "my ugly gosling." Misha was a quiet man; while others were yelling, laughing, and later singing drunkenly, he sat in the corner with one of Sergey's technical magazines. When Raya appeared next to him, always out of nowhere, all flushed, intoxicated by the party atmosphere, he put his hand around her waist in a shy but at the same time proprietary way. She stroked his back, rubbed her face against his bony shoulder, said "You're my ugly gosling," and kissed him, making him blush and smile. Apparently, Galina thought, the ugliness in a man was something you could get used to. Otherwise, Raya wouldn't be able to kiss him, or stroke his back, or go to bed with him and enjoy it.

"Well, I enjoy it," Raya had once said, sitting in Galina's kitchen. "Misha's not bad . . . he does everything to give me pleasure." Raya sat on the windowsill with her feet dangling. Galina was on her knees, scrubbing her chipped wooden floor. The stirring of Raya's shoes in front of her face was very annoying. Then Raya bent down to Galina and said in a slow whisper, "But, you see, something's missing." Galina caught herself blushing all over. She mumbled something like "Really?" and dived under the table to continue scrubbing there.

"How is yours?" Raya asked once. Galina wasn't surprised by her question. She could feel that Raya longed to talk about that every time they chatted about the kids, shopping, and underwear. Galina had even prepared her answer. Deep sigh and shy smile. "I bet," Raya said. "Your husband is so handsome!" Galina heard this a lot. She used to think him handsome too. But with time, Galina started noticing the drawbacks in Sergey's appearance, more and more of them each year, and then nothing but drawbacks. Recently, she'd noticed that with his slightly protruding eyes and meaty lips, Sergey looked like a cow.

"He tries to give her pleasure," Galina often thought, while sitting across from Misha in Raya's kitchen. The very idea of trying to give each other pleasure was strange to Galina. Neither she nor her husband had ever had that intention. At first, when there was passion, they just did it in a way that seemed to be the simplest and the most obvious. They were like two hungry animals that gobble up their food, not bothering to enhance the flavors or to serve it beautifully. And after a few years of marriage, especially since Sergey's drinking had intensified, their infrequent sex had been hardly about pleasure or even simple enjoyment. Sergey usually crawled into bed, sighed, and whispered, "Let's put the stick in." "Some stick!" Galina thought. It was limp and looked more like a wrinkled old sock. It hurt when Sergey struggled to put it in. "Help me," he said plaintively. Galina helped him, trying not to look at his neck, reddened with effort, and his damp hair, unnaturally yellow in the moonlight. After that the bedsprings started squeaking with resentment, and Galina lay, squished by Sergey's heavy body, feeling his unshaven chin rubbing against her skin somewhere above her ear. She sometimes threw worried looks in the direction of Tanya's bed, but Tanya always slept soundly with her face buried between the pillow and the wall. In a few minutes, the squeaking was over and Galina hurried to the bathroom. When she returned, Sergey was fast asleep.

The high point of Galina's sex life came in the gynecologist's office, where she went for her annual checkups. The doctor, an unsmiling women with a thin bun of greasy dark hair, never looked at her patients. She checked them quickly with a slightly disgusted expression, then sat down at her desk and buried herself in her papers. Galina knew that at some point the doctor would cough and ask, "Do you live . . . ?"—inquiring in this modest manner, whether a patient was sexually active. Galina always said yes. She did.

She lived.

GALINA'S LEGS WERE ACHING—she must have walked a long distance. A few feet away, she saw the bright red letters in the sign of the Central Clothing Store. ODEZHDA. Actually, the letters D and E had fallen off, and the sign looked like a mouth with missing teeth. Galina walked to the entrance, stepping over the shards of broken glass. The store's glass window had been broken, and what had been inside stolen or ravaged—the work of looters. She peeked inside, careful not to cut herself on the shards of glass. Torn boxes, pieces of cloth, a few metal dress racks, plastic hangers, and buttons—hundreds of buttons—were scattered all over the stone floor. White plastic dummies stripped of clothes, with their bold heads and gray felt torsos, were lying on their backs by the gaping holes that had once been windows. Further into the store, Galina saw the door to the fitting room hanging on one hinge, and inside the fitting room, a shattered mirror.

That day when Galina and Raya were changing into the identical new dresses in that very fitting room, Galina had been in a hurry to put her dress on, because she didn't want Raya to see her ugly woolen underwear. She threw the dress over her head and wiggled her body to pull it down. The zipper got stuck, and Raya, who was still in her underwear, came up to help. Galina felt Raya's sharp little fingernails tickling her back as she was yanking up the zipper. It was chilly in there, and they were giggling from cold and excitement.

The dresses were made of light cotton, dark blue with specks of white and red. They had short sleeves, low necklines, and fringed hems. "We are twins!" Raya cried when they both looked in the mirror, but Galina saw that the identical dresses, instead of making them more alike, pointed out the differences. Raya's face had more color. Her skin was very white, her cheeks rosy, her blond hair lighter than Galina's, and her eyes were of a brighter shade of blue—Galina's were almost gray. Or maybe it was Raya's beautiful turquoise earrings that made her eyes seem so blue. Galina saw that her own features were regular and well defined, when everything on Raya's face was smooth and diffused: puffy eyelids, plump cheeks without a cheekbone line, soft mouth. Galina tried to figure out what the shape of Raya's nose reminded her of. Then she saw it: a big raindrop, narrow at the top, rounded and wide at the tip. Galina smoothed the folds of fabric over her chest and straightened her back. Her breasts were firm, her shoulders broad, her legs shapely and muscular. Her whole body was finely molded, if a little square. Raya's figure seemed to be made of imperfections. She had thin legs and forearms, but her upper arms and thighs were plump. In addition to that, Galina had seen a glimpse of belly hanging above Raya's silk underpants when they were changing. No matter how elegant and expensive those underpants were, they couldn't conceal the soft white bags of excessive flesh.

Galina was called beautiful more often than Raya. One man in the library even said that she was a pure example of Slavic beauty and that he had seen a painting that looked exactly like Galina in one of the art books. The man was very old. His fluffy white beard touched the pages of the book when he was leafing through it, trying to find the painting for Galina. When he found the page, they saw that it wasn't a painting, but a marble sculpture called simply *A Slavic Woman*. Galina agreed that there was a striking resemblance. The same hard upturned nose, the same prominent cheekbones, the same firm, finely carved lips. The woman from the book was beautiful, and so was Galina. But men always noticed imperfect Raya first. Raya smiled a lot, Raya shrieked, Raya squinted her eyes, Raya painted her lips bright red, Raya rocked her hips, Raya talked sweetly to every man that walked into the library, Raya wore high heels and shiny narrow belts fastened too tight on her plump waist. "A little whore," as Galina's mother would have said.

For some reason, Galina's mother had been turning up in her thoughts more often since the war began. Galina didn't think about her with defiance, the way she used to before her mother's death and for a long time after that; now instead she tried to imagine how her mother would have reacted to one event or another in Galina's life. Galina tried to bring up the memories of the time that they spent together, to recall her mother's words, the sound of her voice, her facial expressions. Most often, she thought of their Easter walks to the cemetery, maybe because that holiday seemed to soften her mother, and that was when Galina felt closest to her. Galina was holding her mother's hand as they walked to the village cemetery along with the cheerful crowd of smartly dressed, drunk, over-heated people, who carried brightly colored paper flowers, dyed eggs, bottles of vodka and Easter cakes. The crowd squeezed through the iron gates, then spilled into the cemetery to eat and drink on the graves of their relatives. The grave she and her mother visited was in the last row, by the fence. There were very few other people in their corner. They spread their food on a little bench set into the soil where Galina's grandparents, her father, and her baby brother had been buried. Galina didn't remember any of them, and she wasn't sad; she liked the gay colors of dyed eggs and paper flowers, the taste of sweet, crumbling cake, the quiet of the place. Galina's mother didn't talk much, except this one time, when she had had a little more to drink. "Look there, Galina," she said, pointing her rough brown hand in the direction of the fence that separated the Christian cemetery from the Jewish. Her face was flushed and her eyes glistened. "Those are Jewish graves. Look at them. And then look at ours." Galina stood up, shaking the crumbs off her starched Easter dress, and walked to the fence. There she moved the dense branches of a young maple tree away from her face and looked. "Look what Jews have, daughter," Galina's mother repeated. She saw iron fences painted black, and inside the fences, fragile shoots of young violets and forget-me-nots struggling through the heavy, dark soil. She saw gravestones— they were small, but made of real stone, each of them with a crooked, wrongly shaped star. "Now look what we have." Galina stepped away from the fence and looked around: lopsided crosses made of rotting wood, paper wreaths, and eggshell, a sea of colored eggshell. On the way back, Galina was tired and sleepy and had to lean on her mother's hip. Her mother's words were coming from above and seemed to bundle up Galina's head like a heavy, warm shawl. "Remember, Galina. Jews get everything. They have ways."

Galina wondered what her mother would have thought if she knew that Galina was hiding Jews in her own home.

ON THE NIGHT when Raya was supposed to leave with the peasant, she appeared at Galina's door at about 3 A.M. She stood in the doorway in her boots caked with country mud, soaked with sweat under her winter coat and shivering. She said that they had come to the road crossing as had been agreed and had waited there until two, but the peasant didn't come. Galina tried hard to hide her initial happy reaction on seeing Raya again. She could barely listen to Raya's words: "I saw Russian troops. They were running. Running!" They were jumping over the fences, she said; most of them didn't even have their guns or rifles. They were trying to tear their uniforms off as they ran. "This is the end," Raya said. "We're going to die." There was a weird, agitated expression on her face. She seemed to be waiting for something. Her eyelids were twitching, and she was rubbing them with the back of her hand. "Calm down. This is not the end," Galina said. They stood in silence for a few minutes.

There were dabs of mud on Galina's spotless doormat after Raya left. Galina picked it up and went to the sink to wash it.

"The Germans will be in town soon, very soon," Galina thought as thin streams of brown water ran into the sink off the dormat. "They may even come today. If you believe the refugees, it will be a matter of days before they'll round up the Jews." Her hands were getting cold; she shook the water off the doormat and carried it back to the hall. "Raya may be dead in a few days," she thought. Both Raya and Leeza. Galina sat down, making the chair screech. Tanya shifted in her sleep, and Galina rose to pull up her blanket. They will be dead unless they come here. Galina's heart was pounding, but her mind suddenly became very clear. Everybody they knew thought that Raya was going to leave with the peasant. Just a few families remained on their street since the evacuation, and there was very little chance that somebody had seen Raya returning tonight. If Raya and Leeza stayed in Galina's back room and never left her apartment, nobody would ever see them. Tanya was very smart for her age; Galina knew that she wouldn't talk. The people who used to drop by Galina's place before the war— mostly Sergey's friends—were all gone. Nobody could inform on them to the Germans. And if the Germans decided to look for Jews in houses, they would hardly make it to Galina's remote part of the town. There still was danger, of course. Great danger. But the thought of the danger didn't dampen Galina's ardor; on the contrary, it made her all the more enthusiastic.

Galina didn't remember ever being as excited as she was, running to Raya's place. They had to make it to her place before dawn. "Grab your things and come to my place. We have to make it before morning," she said breathlessly to Raya as soon as she entered her dark hall. Raya, still fully dressed, but without her coat, rushed up to Galina and burst out sobbing. She mumbled something rapidly while clenching Galina's shoulders. The words coming from her mouth seemed to be drenched with snot. They were hard to make out. They were about the great risk for Galina and Tanya, and that Raya couldn't accept this, that she and Leeza had better try to sneak out of the town, walk to the woods and hide there, and then again about the sacrifice, the great risk for Galina and that she couldn't accept it. Galina felt Raya's sharp chin and sticky tears on her shoulder. She had the urge to dry herself, but she had to wait until Raya was through. She knew that Raya's tears were sincere, but at the same time she sensed that her little speech had been prepared. She glanced around the room and saw Raya's unpacked suitcase by the door, her coat, dropped on the chair, and Leeza, also still fully clothed, hunched in the corner of the sofa. Galina saw that her invitation had been expected for a long time and already accepted. She felt her excitement fading.

Later, Raya and Leeza stood silently in the hall of Galina's apartment. Raya had been at Galina's place hundreds of times before and knew her way around it. When Galina threw birthday parties, Raya, who always came early to help, was rushing from the kitchen to the living room and back, helping Galina to set the table and bring the dishes in. And when the guests came, Raya met them in the hall and told them where to put their coats and led them cheerfully into the living room. Now she stood barefoot on the knitted doormat—she had just taken off her boots—asking where to put Leeza's and her coats. Galina gave them slippers and led them to the back room. They went there timidly and sat on the bed. Tanya, who had been woken up and told everything, sat in her bed, trying hard to look serious and adultlike. Nobody knew what to do next. Galina looked at Leeza's sharp shoulders under a checkered dress, Raya's hands folded between her knees. These two lives were now completely dependent on her; their very existence was in her hands. Galina desperately wanted to back out, to say: "No, no, you can't stay here. It's not for me. I am the wrong type of person. I am not prepared." But it was too late to change anything.

GALINA WALKED AWAY from the clothing store. Her legs and back had become stiff. She made a few hard, quick steps to warm her feet. As she was stomping her feet on the rough surface of the sidewalk, Galina had an unnerving feeling that Raya was somewhere nearby. That she had followed her all the way from home and was standing, hidden somewhere, behind a lamppost or a former beer stall. Galina even took a quick look around, but of course there was nobody there.

A few feet further down, she saw an abandoned tramcar. It stood on the rails with the doors open, as if it had just stopped and was waiting for the passengers to get in. There was something very peaceful about it. Galina walked to the closest door and climbed inside. It didn't bother her that all the light bulbs had been unscrewed and the windows

removed, along with most of the seats. Galina made her
way to the back and sat there on one of the remaining seats.
She thought that if she closed her eyes she might hear the
tramcar's bell and it would start off with a jolt. And then
Raya would start talking. For some reason, when they used
to ride together, Raya talked only when the tram was in
motion. When the tram made stops, Raya also stopped
abruptly and waited until it resumed. That was how Galina
heard about Raya's love affair, between tram stops.

"I think that man likes me," Raya said. Her feverish
whisper was mingled with the rattling wheels and the
crackling of the tram's wires. "That man, from the library,
did you notice him?"

Galina had noticed. A man had come to their corner
and asked if they had some reference books on hydrome-
chanics. A new face in town, probably an engineer on a
business trip. A rather unimpressive man, in his late forties,
short, balding, with a neat, round belly rising above his
trousers belt. Raya blushed and offered to show him the
shelf. She walked ahead of him, and Galina could see that
Raya tried a little too hard to straighten her back and make
her hips rock smoothly. The reference books were on the
upper shelf. Raya had to climb up the ladder. When she
stepped down, the man gave her his hand, but she
stumbled (on purpose, Galina was sure of that) and
laughed as playfully as she could.

Raya wiggled in her seat and sighed: "He has beautiful
eyes, doesn't he? And his mouth . . ."

Ordinary eyes, Galina thought. Small, dark. She tried to remember his mouth. He had full, bright lips, the kind that were usually described as sensual in novels. Did that make him a good kisser? "I wonder how his kisses feel," said Raya, and Galina flinched at the similarity of their thoughts.

And then, when they were squeezing through the crowd to the exit, Raya whispered: "You know what he said to me?" Galina shrugged. Raya leaned close to her and Galina could hear her fast, excited breathing and feel the faint, unpleasant smell of her lipstick. "He said that, when I was standing on the ladder, he could see the contours of my underpants through my dress, and he couldn't take his eyes off them!"

Galina was stunned. She couldn't stop thinking about that all the way home from the tram stop, and later, while she was preparing dinner and waiting for Sergey to come home. Her roommates in college used to talk about their boyfriends all the time, but their talk was coarse and direct: "He came by last night. We fucked." That didn't move or embarrass Galina. This was different. Galina couldn't quite understand how it was different, but she knew that she didn't want to hear it. She couldn't avoid it though. Whenever they got together, at work, during lunch hour, when Raya dropped in for a cup of tea, while riding the tram, Raya talked about her engineer. There were times when she caught Galina's disapproving look, or grin, or flinch. Galina couldn't hide her attitude completely, and Raya wasn't so insensitive as to ignore it, but she simply couldn't stop: she was bursting with stories and details she had to tell; she'd became addicted to telling.

One of Raya's last revelations was made in a tiny café called Meat Patties, where Galina and Raya went on their lunch break. Galina remembered every detail about that day. They stood at the tall, round table with one iron leg—there were no chairs in the café—in front of the big dirty window. Galina had a thick glass in front of her filled with "coffee beverage"—a sweet grayish liquid lacking both coffee flavor and aroma. Raya was holding an identical glass, but filled with beef broth. There was a chipped white plate with two patties on the table along with Raya's shiny black purse. Raya nibbled on her patty, having just told Galina the latest developments in her affair. Then she put the patty down and licked the crumbs off her lips with a dreamy smile. "You know what he told me yesterday?" she asked. Galina silently groaned, preparing to hear another sloppy compliment, but she wasn't prepared for this. "He said"—Raya said it slowly, emphasizing every word—"that my 'you know'"—she glanced down at those words—"tastes like red currant jelly." Then she laughed. Galina felt her whole body go down as if somebody very strong were dragging her to the floor, and at the same time she felt that the heavy, round table was tilting in her direction along with the patties, the glasses, and Raya's purse. She grabbed her glass instinctively, and when her dizzy spell—she figured later that it must have been a dizzy spell—began receding, she found herself still holding tight to her drink and Raya

33

still laughing. The sensation couldn't have lasted more than a few seconds, but Galina felt ill and disoriented. She couldn't bear the sight of laughing Raya with her crooked teeth and the blue slits of her eyes. She suddenly felt an irresistible urge to throw her hot coffee into Raya's face, to hear her laughter replaced by a scream, to see her delicate features distorted by shock and horror, and see the streams of dirty liquid running down her pale cheeks. The urge was so strong that Galina caught herself raising her glass and pointing it in Raya's direction. She didn't throw it; instead, she found herself asking in a strange, coarse voice, feeling that her words weren't her own but dropped out of her mouth like heavy rocks: "Does it?" Raya stopped laughing. "Does it what?" "Taste like red currant jelly?" Raya laughed again, quieter this time: "How would I know?" she said.

That night, it was too hot to sleep. Galina lay in bed on top of the covers, fanning herself with the lacy ruff of her thin cotton nightgown. She could hear her daughter making quiet whistling sounds in her sleep and her husband snoring next to her. Galina tried to imagine how it would feel if a man did all those things to her. She tried to picture the boys who'd courted her in college, but she couldn't remember anything about them. All she saw was blurry gray figures without faces, wearing cheap student clothes. Yet she had a vivid image of Raya's lover, painfully clear as if he were right here in bed with her. Everything that seemed ugly and revolting about him before was arousing now. She could feel his shameless red lips pressing into hers and crawling down her neck, she could feel his big, soft hairy stomach touching her legs. She could feel herself inhaling his unfamiliar breath and pushing up her nightgown for him. She could see his head—balding crown, framed with dark, wiry hair—moving between her legs. Galina slipped her hand down.

She hadn't done so in a long time, not since she was fifteen and her mother caught her at it. She still remembered her mother's coarse scream and her hard, very cold fingers groping her shoulder. She pushed Galina off the bed and dragged her, shivering and stumbling, to their big stone oven, where she grabbed Galina by the wrists and pressed her palms to the red-hot iron door. Galina remembered how afterward she sat on her bed, too shocked to cry, and her mother was greasing her burned palms with lard, crying and saying again and again, "Galina, I don't want you to become a whore."

Galina's eyes were closed, but she felt her mother staring at her now from her picture on the wall. "Yes, Mother, yes," Galina thought, "look what I am doing! Maybe I want to be a whore. Maybe that's what I've always wanted!"

When it was over, Galina pushed back the damp bangs that stuck to her face and wiped the beads of sweat from her nose. Her hands were trembling and her heart was beating so fast that it nauseated her. Her mother's picture was barely visible in the moonlight, but still Galina could make out her tightly pressed thin lips, her carefully combed hair parted in the middle, and her eyes. She suddenly noticed that her mother didn't have her usual severe expression in that photograph. She looked bewildered, as if a photographer had taken her by surprise; she looked frightened. Galina turned onto her side. The whistling sounds that her daughter made drove her crazy, like the buzzing of a bunch of mosquitoes. So did Sergey's bursts of snoring. He lay on his back now. His mouth was agape. He reeked of onions and vodka. Galina buried her head under a pillow and sobbed.

The next morning, she was late for work. She woke up on time, but she lingered at home trying to put off the moment when she would have to see Raya. She knew that she wouldn't be able to listen to her stories today. Galina saw Sergey off to work and Tanya off to school, then went back to bed. She lay wrapped in a thick woolen blanket and thought about Raya. Her thoughts were different than before. They were full of hatred. She had felt some resentment or envy or maybe even anger before, but never this. She lay and wished that the most horrible things would happen to Raya. She wished that her husband would know about her affair and throw her out. She imagined Misha's long, awkward body shaking with sobs. She imagined pale, scrawny Leeza holding her father's hand, trying to comfort him. And she imagined Raya, on her knees in a doorway, begging them to let her stay. Misha wouldn't even look in her direction, and Leeza would only shake her head no. Maybe Misha would receive a letter from somebody telling him about the affair, or a phone call. A phone call would be better. Somebody should call him. It was so easy to pick up the phone and dial the number . . . Galina felt a cold sweat breaking out on her forehead. Maybe she was simply coming down with something. Maybe she had a fever. She took a little thermometer out of the bedside drawer, shook it, and stuck it under her arm. Five minutes later, she inspected it and saw that her temperature was normal. Galina climbed off the bed and dragged herself to the bathroom. She turned on cold water and held her face under the tap for a few seconds, then she began dressing for work.

Raya wasn't at her desk. It was the first thing that Galina noticed when she walked into the library. The desk looked deserted, with Raya's broken pencils in the pink plastic cup and a small family photo, but without her scattered lollipops, the shiny purse, and her knitted cardigan thrown on the chair's back. For a second, Galina thought that her wishes had come true, that something horrible happened, that Raya's husband found out and that somehow it was all Galina's fault. Then the women in the library told her that Raya was okay, just taking a sick day to sit with her daughter. Galina felt relief at first, but then it became relief mixed with disappointment. Raya wasn't punished. "She got away," Galina thought. "She can have all she wants and get away with it."

A few days later, Raya came back. She looked thinner, had dark circles under her eyes, and smiled less. She said that her daughter had had a bad cold and the doctors suspected pneumonia, but the diagnosis wasn't confirmed. Then Raya added matter-of-factly that the engineer had gone back to Moscow and that she didn't care. "When your child is sick, you can't be bothered with this stuff." Galina could see that Raya was lying. She could see how tense Raya became every time the phone rang in the library, how she stared at the same spot on her desk until somebody answered the call and she heard that it wasn't for her. Raya didn't laugh as much as she had before. She didn't flirt with men—when they walked up to her table, she gave them a quick, sulky look the way all the library employees did. "He dumped her," Galina thought, liking the sound of the word. "Dumped, dumped, dumped." A rubber ball bouncing against the ground. The resentment and hatred were fading away. Galina felt as if she had recovered from a bad, exhausting illness. She could breathe again, she could look at Raya, she could talk to her again.

GALINA GOT OUT of the tramcar. She didn't know where she wanted to go. She thought of turning right and continuing to walk on tree-lined Chkalov Street, and she even took a few steps in that direction, but something made her change her mind and continue walking along the tramline, toward the City Hall. The street ran down the hill; it was easier to walk and Galina walked faster.

Was there a single moment when this present chilliness between her and Raya had started? Now it seemed that their relationship wasn't descending smoothly, but lurching downward by tugs the way a rusty old elevator does. A lurch—a stop—a lurch—a stop.

The first lurch happened because of that ridiculous business of praying for their husbands. There had been no news or letters from the front. The girls asked questions at first, but then they stopped. They understood. They didn't mention their fathers, and if they did, accidentally, they immediately stopped and exchanged panicky looks, as if they thought that the lives of their fathers were so fragile right now that anything, even saying their names aloud, could destroy them. Galina and Raya did not mention their husbands either. They agreed that the subject would be too upsetting. But Galina wondered if the true reason for their silence was the fear of insincerity.

The prayers had been started by the girls. Galina didn't know who had the idea, Tanya or Leeza. Neither of them knew how to pray. They had never been in church and never heard anybody pray at home. Their pleas sounded more like Christmas wishes: "Kind, dear God, please, don't let my father die." For a few evenings, Galina and Raya just watched the girls. They watched their little bodies rocking softly, while their mouths eagerly breathed out naïve words of prayer. Their eyes were directed somewhere upward, as if there, on Galina's whitewashed ceiling, was the figure of God, visible only to them.

One evening, after the girls had gone to sleep, Raya suggested that she and Galina pray too. She looked embarrassed when she said it. She was playing with the fringe on the tablecloth and avoided looking at Galina. Raya said that she didn't believe in God and didn't know how to pray, but maybe it would make her feel better. Galina shrugged. They got down on their knees, making the rough floorboards creak, and stayed in these awkward poses, not knowing what to say. Raya was the first to begin; she started the way the girls did. "Dear God . . ." Galina had often heard her mother pray, and she'd even been in church with her once or twice, but she couldn't remember any words—just "Amen," which her mother used at the end, before she got up from her knees, groaning and crossing herself. Galina had to fill the gap between "Dear God" and "Amen" somehow. She tried to invoke warm feelings about her husband, but instead she caught herself blaming him. She thought that it was his fault that they had stayed in the town. It was his fault that he'd been kicked out of the Party. "Engaged in inappropriate behavior! Some rebel!" Galina thought. She knew that he had simply showed up drunk at one of the Party committee meetings and that it wasn't the first time. She remembered how he spent all their money on vodka. She remembered how, when he couldn't find the money, he took things from home and sold them at the flea market. He sold Galina's favorite lamp, the one with a blue velvet shade. She tried harder to find some forgiveness. She tried to think about Sergey the way Tanya did. Tanya, who always rushed to her father when he came home drunk, helped him to undress, stroked his puffy, apologetic face, and said, when he slipped and fell, "It's okay, Daddy, the floor is slippery. We just washed it." How could Tanya treat him this way, when it was the money for her coat that he stole and spent? He would come back from the front and steal more money, and they would have to continue living like that. Galina felt bitter, angry tears coming up her throat. Could it be that she didn't want Sergey to come back? Could it be that she wanted him to die? The thought startled her. She felt her heart pounding heavily against her rib cage, hurting her, as if it were made of stone. She turned to look at Raya. She was kneeling with her head bent low. Her tightly shut eyelids were trembling, her chapped lips moving eagerly; she licked them with a swift movement from time to time. Galina watched her, feeling that her own guilt was fading, making a place for her resentment of Raya: "Some faithful little wife!"

The next night, Galina said that she didn't feel like praying. So they didn't do it again. And soon their prewar recollections stopped too. That was when Raya began writing letters to her husband every night. Just a few tortured lines, with words crossed out, written over, then crossed out again. She often turned to glance in Galina's direction, and it was then that her expression became frightened. But they were still talking. Not as much as before and not as easily, but not yet the complete silence of recent weeks.

Galina felt that something sharp was in her right boot. It was rolling under her foot, hurting her when she occasionally stepped on it. She limped to a lamppost. There she leaned on the cold concrete pole and removed her boot, reaching with her hand into the boot's warm, damp inside to pull out a tiny jagged rock. It must have been a piece of gravel from her walk along the rails. She pulled the boot back on and moved her numbed toes.

She knew why they had stopped talking. It was because of Raya's earrings. Galina could close her eyes and see them now. They were the most beautiful things she had ever seen. Small, elongated pieces of turquoise, shaped like large raindrops, hanging on thin golden threads with tiny curved golden petals connecting the turquoise drop to the thread. Raya used to wear them every day, even with the clothes that didn't match their exquisite blue color. She said that without the earrings she looked naked. "And ugly, and old," she added, laughing. She had taken them off that night when she and Leeza were supposed to leave town with the peasant. And it was true that without them Raya's face looked naked and drawn of color. Without the earrings, Galina could see that Raya's pale skin had a grayish tone and that her ears were too big for her face. Galina wondered what had happened to the earrings—had Raya hidden them somewhere, or did she have them with her. Until the day she saw them again.

It happened a few days after their attempt at praying. Raya came out of the back room with a tiny bundle, something gray and fuzzy. She was holding it carefully on her outstretched palm as if it were a baby bird. When she got closer to Galina, Galina saw that it was not a bundle but an old woolen mitten. Raya reached inside and pulled out a faded matchbox. Galina guessed what was inside before Raya opened it, but still, seeing the earrings in all their brilliance here, against the shabby surface of the matchbox, was shocking. Galina could see that it was shocking to Raya too. They stared at the earrings for a few seconds, then Raya said, stretching her lips into a smile: "I thought maybe you could exchange them for milk? Or cream? Leeza's cough has been bad lately." She touched the earrings, running her translucent fingers along the thin veins in the turquoise. "It's light turquoise and gold—they used to be expensive."

So Galina took them to their little town market. She carried them the same way, in a matchbox wrapped in the mitten. She squeezed past rows of peasant women in long, thick skirts and gray shawls. They were holding bushels of eggs with dried-up chicken droppings stuck to them, coarse gray loaves of bread, and shriveled potatoes. They had sleek faces and shrewd little eyes. And there were rows of women in urban clothes with pitiful pieces of jewelry dangling in their pale fingers. Earrings, cheap necklaces, thin wedding rings, men's watches. These women had long faces and desperate, begging eyes. Galina passed them quickly and went to the end of the row, where she often saw a farmer woman selling milk. There she was, a short woman with a fat, oily face under a filthy headscarf. There were two big aluminum milk cans by her feet and a clay jar covered with a piece of cloth in her hands. "Cream," said the woman to Galina in an intimate whisper. Galina looked at the woman's hands; she had cutoff woolen gloves on, and her fingers were fat and red, with dirt under the fingernails. Galina imagined Raya's earrings in these hands, and how the woman would try to fasten them with her swollen fingers. Then she imagined the earrings dangling on their golden threads next to the woman's greasy cheeks. She knew it was unlikely that the woman would wear the earrings herself; she would probably wait for better times and sell them, but still she felt that she wouldn't be able to bear seeing the earrings in the woman's hands even during the brief moment of transaction. She put her hand into her coat pocket and pushed the mitten with the earrings further down. She acquired the jar of cream in exchange for a bar of soap that she carried in her other pocket.

As she walked back from the market, Galina knew that she wouldn't tell Raya about the earrings. She would tell her that she had sold them. She would come home and hide them in her drawer between stacks of her flannel sheets. There was one woman on the market selling a mirror. Galina stopped there, unwrapped the package quickly, and held the earrings against her ears. She was in such a hurry to wrap them back up that she only saw a glimpse of her reflection, her rigid face instantly brightened by two light-blue spots. All the way home, Galina told herself that she hadn't done anything wrong. After all, Raya and Leeza ate her supplies of food. And they lived at her home. And she had paid for the cream with her bar of soap. The earrings were a small price. She had the right to them. Galina kept fingering the package all the way home. Every time she touched the soft, fuzzy surface of the mitten and the hard edge of the matchbox underneath, she felt a thrill, a titillating feeling of getting away with something.

Her elevated mood vanished as soon as she saw Raya's face. As soon as she saw that Raya knew. Raya rushed to the jar of cream, showering Galina with praises, repeating that the cream would save Leeza's life, displaying exaggerated gratitude to the point where it began making Galina dizzy. Raya's behavior was made up of two strands, contradictory and sickening. The first was to show that she never, not for a moment, could suppose that Galina hadn't sold the earrings. The second was to show that if Galina did take the earrings, Raya didn't mind; on the contrary, she was happy that Galina might have done that, it was Galina's right to do that, Galina risked her life for them and the earrings were such a small price. Galina went to the kitchen, pretending that she had things to do there. She began scrubbing the pots that she hadn't used in months with her trembling hands. If only Raya could shut up!

Later that day, Galina came to a realization. She watched how Raya tried to feed the warmed-up cream to Leeza. "Please, darling, please, it'll make you feel better." Leeza swallowed it spoon by spoon slowly, reluctantly. At one moment she choked and began coughing, and Raya patted her on the back, while throwing a nervous glance in Galina's direction. She wanted Galina to take the earrings! Maybe she had even made it all up—made up the whole story about milk for Leeza—to make Galina take the earrings. Galina felt a heavy, cold wave of nausea. She had to grab a doorframe to keep her balance. Raya wanted to bribe her. Galina went back to the kitchen and sank down on the low stool. She wanted to bribe her! Why? Because she was afraid that Galina would ask her to go? Or worse, because she was afraid that Galina would walk downtown and tell the Germans that there were Jews in her house. No, that was ridiculous, the Germans would kill her and Tanya if they knew that they were giving shelter to Jews. Or would they? She could always say that they had been hiding somewhere else, that they had just come to her place to ask for shelter or for food, and she immediately went to report it. Nobody would be interested in finding out the truth, and nobody there would listen to Raya. These thoughts startled Galina. What was happening? Was she just trying to unravel Raya's way of thinking, or was she really considering going to the Germans? She took a cold teakettle off the stove and began drinking hungrily right out of its rough tin spout. The streams of water ran down her chin and her neck, causing her skin to break out in goose bumps.

THE TRAMLINE MADE a sharp turn on the crossing. It was the first time since the beginning of the occupation that Galina had gone so far downtown. It had gotten considerably darker since she left the house; soon she would have to turn back to make it on time before the curfew. Or she could walk the last two or three blocks toward the City Hall. Lately, whenever she went to the market, which was not so far from downtown, she had the urge to turn in the City Hall direction. She couldn't understand what it was that attracted her to that place. Galina had no desire to see the Germans. She despised all those women who rushed to the center in the first days of occupation to see what Germans looked like. They even looked up some German words in a dictionary so they would be able to introduce themselves. Galina saw one girl from the library, a freckled Masha, bending over a German phrasebook and repeating over and over, *"Ich heisse Mascha,"* her thin lips making a funny circle when she said *"Ich."*

Galina wondered how much German she remembered. She had good grades in high school, but it had been more than ten years since she'd held a German textbook in her hands. *"Hier ist ein Tisch." "Das Wetter ist schön heute."* It was strange how these expressions, buried in her memory for so many years, were now coming to surface. Galina made another effort. *"Gretchen geht nach Schule."* She smiled. German words were rolling under her tongue like sucking candies. She tried to apply some of the expressions to herself. *"Ich heisse Galina"; "Galina geht nach Schule."* She wondered if her lips looked as funny as Masha's. How did they say "How are you"? *"Ich geht . . ."* No, no . . . *"Wie geht es Ihnen?"* Something like that.

Galina forgot about her tired, aching legs. She walked briskly to the brightly lit City Hall plaza. The German words were floating up in her head one after another, forming sentences and whole conversations:

Hello. Wie geht es Ihnen?
Danke gut. Und ihnen?
Danke auch gut. *Ich heisse Galina.* Es gibt Juden in mein Haus.

Galina's heart skipped a beat, then began pounding wildly. She took off her headscarf and unbuttoned her jacket. *Es gibt Juden in mein Haus. Es gibt Juden in mein Haus. Es gibt Juden in mein Haus.* The words seemed glued to her lips. They were burning her, scorching the inside of her mouth and further down her throat. She didn't really want to say those words. She couldn't. But what if she could? Galina saw that she was very close to the City Hall plaza now. She could see lights coming from the shabby brick building of the former City Hall. She could see German vehicles. She could hear the whirring of motors. If she took just a few more steps, she would have been able to hear real German speech, not just the textbook variations.

Galina turned around and started running in the opposite direction. She ran very fast, as if the Germans were chasing her, her white headscarf streaming in the wind like a flag. She couldn't want to do that. It wasn't true. It was all because of Raya! Raya had pushed her. Raya was distrustful and ungrateful. Raya would have never done for Galina what Galina was doing for her. Galina was a good person. She was risking her own and her daughter's life to save Raya and Leeza. Galina felt that she couldn't run anymore, she was out of breath. Somehow words about risking her life never moved her. She couldn't make herself feel that she was doing something heroic. Maybe that was because she didn't feel fear. She knew how dangerous it was to hide Jews in her house; she knew that there was a war going on and that people in occupied towns could be killed for lesser crimes; but something prevented her from imagining that she or Tanya could be killed or even hurt. And she couldn't fear anything that she couldn't vividly imagine. She wished that she could.

THEIR STAIRCASE WAS COMPLETELY DARK, and Galina had to fumble with her hand on the wall to find the door. She hoped that Raya wouldn't come out of her room. If

Raya saw Galina's face, she would guess her thoughts, the same way she knew about the earrings. She would know about *"Es gibt Juden in mein Haus."* Galina knocked on the wooden frame four times before opening the door with her key. Raya had asked Galina to do that.

It was very quiet inside. There was only Tanya in the room playing with the doll at the table. The door of the back room was closed. "They're sleeping," Galina thought with relief and went to the sink to wash the mud off her boots. Only when she came out of the bathroom did Galina notice Tanya's blank stare and that she wasn't playing with the doll but simply holding it in her hands, upside down. "Why are you not in bed? Are they sleeping?" Galina asked. Tanya shook her head. "They're gone," she said. Galina walked to the table, the dripping boots still clutched in her hands. The foolish, irrational questions were pouring out of her mouth: "What do you mean 'gone'? Where? When did they leave? Why do you have the doll? Did they say anything?" Then she heard herself screaming: "What do you mean 'gone'?!" Tanya walked to her bed and began undressing. She spoke in an odd, tired voice: "They got dressed and left right after you left. Leeza said she wouldn't need the doll anymore." Tanya paused. "What did she mean? What did Aunt Raya say? Did Raya say anything? Why wouldn't Leeza need the doll?"

Tanya stood by the bed in her white underpants and white undershirt, silently folding her clothes. Then she put her dress on a chair, her ribbed brown tights on top of it, and turned off the light.

Galina slumped on a chair in the dark and sat listening to the creaking of Tanya's wooden bed as she climbed in, to the rustle of the sheets, to Tanya's long, muffled sobbing—she must have had a pillow over her head—and then to the sounds of her breathing gradually getting soft and quiet. Galina thought of the questions that Tanya couldn't stop asking before Raya and Leeza came to live with them. "How do they catch Jews? Do they chase them? Do they use ropes? Does it hurt when they burn them? Do they become all black and shriveled like burned firewood? Does it hurt a lot?"

Galina stood up and tiptoed to Tanya's bed. The pillow was still on her head. Galina gently lifted up her head and put the pillow under it. She looked at Tanya's shoulders—strong tanned shoulders, so much like her own. Galina looked at the round white scar on Tanya's upper arm, just below her shoulder bone. She reached out with her hand and stroked her daughter awkwardly. Tanya flinched in her sleep and pulled her shoulder under the blanket. Galina tiptoed away from the bed. She stumbled on something by the table. Something that made her heart stop beating. Something cold, both hard and soft, with hair. "A dead child," flashed the thought in Galina's head. She couldn't breathe, she couldn't bring herself to look down, she couldn't move her foot.

Then she looked down and saw the contours of Leeza's doll, barely visible in the dark.

Ovrashki's Trains

WHEN I WAS FIVE, we spent the summer in a village with the funny name Ovrashki, thirty miles from Moscow. We rented two tiny rooms in a large green house with carved white shutters of which I always said, "Our house has white lace on the windows." The house stood about fifty feet from the railroad station, and its address was 1 Station Street. Everybody who came to Ovrashki by train had to pass it.

We slept in a narrow room where the only furniture was the four identical iron beds for me, my mother, my grandmother, and my grandfather. The only window was blocked by a lilac bush that kept out the moonlight, leaving the house very dark at night. I was often awakened by the sound of trains. Once each night, a heavy freight train passed our house with a scary rumble. The trains moved slowly, and it took them forever to get through Ovrashki. I could hear the rails groan, and I imagined them sagging more and more and finally cracking, sending the train cars crashing into our house. I thought that I could save myself if I held on to the bed really tight. I lay clutching the bed railing with increasingly damp fingers until the train sounds faded away, and my heart pounded for a long time after that, keeping me from falling asleep. Yet I loved the light suburban trains that swept past at night with whistles and a jolly rattle of wheels. The house would shake slightly, and the iron knobs on our bed frames jingled like little bells and dishes clattered in the kitchen. Sometimes, I brought aluminum spoons into the room, laid them on the wooden floor, and watched them tremble and tinkle as a train passed. I had the idea that my father would come home on one of the suburban trains. He had been abroad on a business trip for a long time. So long, in fact, that I couldn't remember his face or the sound of his voice. Nobody knew the exact date when he was coming home, neither my mother nor my grandmother. But I was somehow sure that he would come home this summer. First he would go to a seaport town on a big white ship with a red flag and blue letters on its side (I'd seen a picture of him on a ship like this). Then he would fly to Moscow. Then he would take a train and come to Ovrashki. But not at night. I thought he would only come in the early evening with the crowd of rush-hour passengers.

All days in Ovrashki seemed alike. I had to be outside as much as possible so I could breathe a lot of fresh air and store it in me for the winter months. Mornings we usually spent at the beach. Ovrashki's beach was a narrow strip of clay soil with small patches of grass, separating the tiny brown lake from the road. If I didn't have a cold, or I wasn't recovering from a cold or about to get a cold, I was allowed to splash in the water. At other times I just sat on a thin, shabby piece of cloth, cut from an old bedcover, munching on carrots and apples, and watched other kids splash in the water. Between ten and noon, cross-country trains passed Ovrashki. The railroad was only a few feet away from the beach, and tired-looking passengers stuck their heads out the train windows. Some of them lay on upper berths, others sat at tables, and I could see glasses of tea in steel glass-holders and hard-boiled eggs in their hands. I wished I could be on one of those trains. I didn't dream of going to strange new places; I just wanted to lie on a hard patent leather berth and sip hot strong tea from a glass in a steel glass-holder. "Wave to them," my mother urged me. "These people are going all the way to Siberia. They must be tired and bored." I waved to them until my wrist began to hurt. Some of them smiled and waved back.

For the rest of the day, after we came back from the beach, I played in the backyard. The house was big and sturdy. Our landlord, Pyotr Ignatievich, was also big and sturdy. He and his wife occupied the largest section of the house, and the rest belonged to his two brothers and their families. The garden was vast and dark, with thick bushes of lilac and jasmine, old apple trees, and weedy vegetable plots. I never grew bored playing alone. The lilac bush was my castle, where I spent long years embroidering (piercing leaves with a stick) while waiting for a prince to come and marry me. The pile of dirt under the porch was my kitchen, or my country shop where I sold dirt pies to my dolls. The rusty pavilion twined with wild grapes was a high-rise building, where I lived with my crippled alcoholic husband and thirteen sons, having to bear their violent tempers. Or sometimes the pavilion served as a TV studio, and I was the host of a talk show.

At about 6 P.M., I dropped whatever I was doing and ran to the fence to meet the Moscow trains. Our dark green fence was the tallest and sturdiest in the village. The boards were set side by side, but between my family's vegetable garden and the wooden outhouse there was a spot where a gap between boards allowed you to see the road. I knew it was close to six o'clock when Pyotr Ignatievich came home from work. He rode his bicycle to the gate, jumped gracefully to the ground, and wheeled the bicycle into the barn. Then he wiped the sweat off his red, creased face and walked slowly to the house, greeting me seriously, without a smile. He always wore his working clothes: soft gray pants and a jacket. As soon as he disappeared into his part of the house, I rushed to the fence. I made my way between the two tall apple trees, feeling small, hard apples under my feet, then I had to step over our lettuce and carrot patches (careful not to ruin them) and climb over the pile of firewood before reaching my watching spot at last.

By the fence, I climbed over a log and sat down, then dug holes in the dirt or played with a caterpillar until I heard the sound of a train. If a whistle followed by "choo-choo-choo" came from the left, I knew that it was a

Moscow-bound train, and I never turned to look. But when it came from the right, I immediately stood up on the log and stuck my face between the thick, uneven boards of the fence.

After the "choo-choo-chooing" slowed down, I heard the brakes screech and the doors open with a long, loud sigh. In a few seconds, the first passengers appeared on the road, hurrying to their homes. They were usually young men who could get ahead of the others because they didn't have any bags. Most of them wore dusty tennis shoes, dark pants, and white nylon shirts. Their hair was blowing and their eyes looked straight ahead, never down at the road or sideways at the houses they passed. In a few minutes, the bag crowd followed. Tired, sweaty, in crumpled clothes, these men and women trudged down the street to their homes. The women had swollen ankles with shoe straps cutting deep into their flesh; the men had large wet spots on the backs of their shirts. This group always stared at their feet, as if their eyes were weighed down by the load of the countless bags stuffed with food they had to bring. They carried watermelons, darkened cabbage, tubes of hard sausage, leaking cartons of milk, bottles of mineral water, cakes in crumpled boxes, but mostly chickens. I was afraid of those chickens with their yellow feet dangling from string-bags, and their bobbing bluish heads with dead eyes, but I couldn't turn away because I didn't want to miss my father. I waited until all of the passengers were gone, and even then I didn't leave my post because sometimes there were two or three straggling behind who couldn't walk as fast as the others. They toiled along the road, making frequent stops to catch their breath.

After the last passenger passed, I jumped down from the log. I had to return to digging in the dirt or playing with a caterpillar until the next train came. Usually, nobody bothered me. My mother was shut in the room, bent over her typewriter, hidden behind a pile of papers. My grandfather was snoring on his bed. My grandmother was either in the kitchen cooking dinner or sitting on the porch engrossed in a book. When she bent her neck to read, her long white bangs fell over her face.

People only passed me on their way to the outhouse. I didn't see anything wrong with waiting for my father, but I didn't want anyone to know what I was doing. I had to pretend to be busy with the vegetable plot. As soon as I saw somebody approaching, I squatted by the garden and pretended to pull out weeds. I hated weeding, because when I pulled out a single weed it always dragged with it a string of good vegetables.

When Pyotr Ignatievich passed by, I ducked my head, hoping that he wouldn't see me. He always made me feel guilty, praising me for weeding the garden when I wasn't really weeding it. I also tried to avoid his wife, Nina Ivanovna. I ducked my head so low that delicate carrot tops tickled my nose, and I could smell fresh soil, dill, and parsley. Nina Ivanovna was fat and short. When she scurried to the toilet, her large breasts, which showed above her tight, low-cut dresses, bounced like footballs, the skin of her bosom greasy and yellow. I once asked her why her breasts were so yellow, and she went into a laughing fit. She told this story to everybody over and over again. "What a smart girl! Pays attention to breasts already!" Every time Nina Ivanovna passed me, she winked and asked, "Want to know why my breasts are so yellow?"

If the weather was nice, I met all six of the evening trains. On rainy nights I had to stay home. I wasn't worried that I might miss my father. I thought that trains didn't run in bad weather. Maybe I had this idea because the rain drumming on the tin roof and our single window drowned out the sound of the trains.

While it was pouring outside, we all occupied our beds. Everyone settled down with a book. My grandfather lay on his back reading memoirs by one of the Russian revolutionaries. He wore an undershirt and dark pants with striped suspenders. As he read, he made grunting and whistling sounds to disagree with the book. After a while, the heavy volume started slipping onto his hairy chest, and soon we could hear his angry snoring, as if he were still arguing with the author. My grandmother lay quietly on her side with a novel. My mother sat up in bed bending over one of her scientific books. Whenever I turned to her, I saw her hunched back, clad in the old navy sweater she wore every day, as she fiercely underlined something or made notes in the book. I found it very unfair that she was allowed to write in books while I was punished for the same thing. I had to leaf through an old picture book and wait for the rain to end. I waited until the gushing of water on the roof slowed down and finally became separate rain-drops. Then I was allowed to go outside.

I pulled on my old rubber boots, which were a little too tight around the toes, and my shiny bright blue raincoat. I splashed down the steps and ran into the garden that smelled of jasmine and rain. I squished in the mud between the vegetable patches, and when I stepped over them, wet leaves of lettuce brushed against my bare calves. The log that I liked to stand on was slippery, and I had to hold on to the darkened boards of the fence.

The train passengers walked faster after the rain, curs-ing when they stepped into puddles. Their bags were soggy, and even the people themselves seemed soggy. The young men shivered in their light shirts.

I was sure I would recognize my father at once. I imag-ined him wearing a dark blue suit, a white shirt, and a tie. In Moscow, I'd once overheard my mother say of him, "David was wearing a dark blue suit and a white shirt to the conference. I couldn't resist running my hand through his hair before he left." She used the word "dashing" to describe him. I thought then that "dashing" meant "very smart." In our Moscow apartment a small black-and-white picture of my father stood in a simple frame on the upper shelf of my mother's bookcase, along with some other objects belong-ing to him. I wasn't allowed to touch any of them, but of course I did when nobody was home. I carried my little wooden chair close to my mother's black desk and climbed on top. I had to be careful because its polished surface was slippery; once I'd slipped and fallen. From the desktop, I reached for the upper shelf of the bookcase, cautiously pulled aside the glass doors, and took out the forbidden objects one by one. To the left was a neat pile of books that my father had written. I knew that he studied the ocean. It was about the only thing I was told about my father. I expected his books to contain a lot of glossy pictures of water, large waves, and sea animals, but there was nothing but formulas, diagrams, and very small letters. Only the covers looked pretty: dark blue with large golden letters.

Then there were two large seashells. I put them to my ears and pressed so tight that it hurt, but I didn't hear a thing. I thought maybe the sea had been in there before but then had seeped out. There also was a little toy bunny. I couldn't understand what he was doing there. He was probably the toy my father was saving for me. I knew that my mother bought toys for me in advance and saved them for my birthday. The bunny was gray with a pink nose and bright red eyes. Its fur looked old and tangled. I stroked the bunny's back, feeling sorry for him. The most forbidden object was kept in a ribbed leather case in the farthest corner of the shelf. I took it out only once. I blew the dust off, unclasped the case, and peeked inside with caution. There was something smooth and round inside, with a spiral-shaped knife and a neatly folded cord: an electric razor, I guessed, though it didn't look like my brother's or grandfather's razor. I pulled it from its case and held it tight as I jumped down to the floor, then walked over to the wall socket. The thing that I was about to do was so scary that I kept licking my lips. I moved the cord slowly toward the socket and plugged it in. Immediately, the razor started bouncing in my hand with a buzzing that was getting louder and louder. I screamed and threw it on the floor. The cord came unplugged, and the buzzing stopped. I thought that my father must be very brave to shave with this thing.

The picture I always saved for last. I wiped the dust off the glass frame with my sleeve and looked at my father's face. He had a large nose, thick dark hair, and he was smiling, but not at me. His eyes were focused on something in the distance.

I planned to run to the gate and open it for my father when I saw him through the fence. Pyotr Ignatievich had put a heavy wooden latch on the gate. I often practiced opening it to make sure I could manage it when my father came. I would open the door and wait for him to come in, because I wasn't allowed to go out into the street.

When the last train passed each day and my father didn't come, I wasn't upset. I knew that there would be more trains tomorrow. Right about that time, my grandmother called me in for dinner. I ran into the long, dark hall where we ate. My grandmother was the only one who talked during dinner. My grandfather was groggy from sleep, and my mother always seemed distracted. I kept blowing on my mashed potatoes and watching my grandfather's head. His seat was under the shelf where my grandmother put dishes to dry, and from time to time a drop of water fell on the bald spot on his crown. That made him grumble and frown, but he never changed his seat. I giggled every time that happened.

Some days that summer passed very quickly. I woke up and was having breakfast, yawning and stretching, and in what seemed a few moments I was already having my milk before going to bed, also yawning. Other days stretched on endlessly. In September, we had to return to Moscow. Several long months passed before I turned six, old enough to learn that my father had died four years earlier from a heart attack. My mother couldn't bear to tell me. She asked her brother to come visit and talk to me. We were sitting on the couch in my room, my uncle was staring at the floor, and I was staring at his shiny forehead, large round nose, and bushy brows. Then he told me something. I didn't understand what he said, because I was thinking of plucking a hair out of his brow. He had to tell me again, and when he did, I started crying. Soon my nose was running and I was wiping it all over my cheeks. My uncle handed me his checkered handkerchief. It was very big, larger than my face, and itchy.

My father died in a little town on the Black Sea, where the sky and sea were of the same cobalt-blue color and the ships that came into the harbor looked startlingly white in a blinding southern sun. The coffin with my father's body traveled to Moscow on a freight train, in a dark car made of thick red boards knocked together, along with some factory equipment in plywood boxes. When the train moved, the car tilted, and the boxes slid down to the side, knocking against the coffin's edge with a hollow sound muffled by the rumble of the train.

I didn't know any of this until years later.

WE SPENT the following summer in Ovrashki again. Every night the Moscow trains stopped at the railroad station, letting out a crowd of tired, sweaty people. When I saw Pyotr Ignatievich step off his bike, I ran through the garden to the porch, which was as far as you could get from the fence. I crawled under the thick boards smelling of rotten wood, and sat on a white brick sticking out from the foundation. Light shined down through the porch steps in four stripes. I dug out the fat, black soil with my hands, kneaded it, and formed little pies to put into my plastic toy dishes. Yet from under the house I could still hear the muffled sounds of trains. When the train whistle blew, I pressed my hands tight to my ears and waited for what seemed like a lifetime for the sounds to die out. Invariably, when I came to dinner, someone would wonder how I'd managed to have traces of soil on my ears.

Lydia's Grove

To get to Lydia's Grove, in the southwest corner of Moscow, my mother and I had to take a bus and a subway. That winter we traveled there almost every week. We waited for the bus inside a rusty iron shed surrounded by piles of hardened gray December snow. My mother kept stepping out of the shed to look for the bus, hugging herself and asking me if I was warm enough. I wasn't warm, I was hot, in felt boots, bulky fur coat—too childish for an eight-year-old—and a knitted hat that cut into my Vaselined cheeks. Only my hands were cold. I never wore mittens, though, because I needed my fingers to be free. I could hardly move under all those layers of clothing; I would have felt completely helpless with my fingers stuck in thick woolen mittens.

When the bus came, my mother pressed her heavy bag to her chest, grabbed me with her free hand, and made her way through the crowd to take a seat by the heating grill.

I brought my reddened, numb fingers close to the heater, feeling how its ticklish warmth slowly unfroze them, then pressed my forehead to the iced window to thaw out a looking spot. Through that spot, I could see the familiar gray road surrounded by wilted trees, grayish-white school buildings, identical supermarkets with dirty windows, Party slogans written in dirty white letters on faded red boards, and nine-story gray apartment buildings—all of them were long, some stretched for miles. People called them "fallen skyscrapers." On the side of one of those long buildings, there was a twenty-foot-high portrait of Lenin. It looked like the head of a gigantic caterpillar.

Once we transferred to the subway, we always tried to take the spot on a two-seat bench in the corner. "We can have some privacy here," my mother said. She undid the top buttons of her and my coats, put the bag onto her lap, and took out the greasy, badly typed pages of her manuscript. She had to do more revisions before meeting with Lydia Petrovna Rousseau. They wrote children's books together. For years, their names had appeared on their book jackets with a hyphen: Veller-Rousseau. Some of their readers even thought that it was one person with a double name.

Having nothing to do, I usually watched my mother on the train. Her face looked beautiful under a beige fur hat. She had a small nose, thick black brows, and big brown eyes. "The eyes of a horse," as I had once said, intending it as a compliment; horses do have beautiful eyes. Her hands weren't beautiful—they were rough, with bulging veins and wrinkled red fingers covered with ink. On her middle finger, she still wore a simple wedding band, although my father had died many years before.

As the train approached the center of Moscow, more people squeezed themselves into the car, carrying food, rolled up rugs, window frames, skis, backpacks, wooden boxes. I tried to push myself back into the seat as far as possible, but I still felt trapped under dripping bags and heated bodies in winter coats. I knew all the stops and counted them. Our stop was twenty-second. Actually, it was simply called Southwest. Only my mother called it Lydia's Grove, because of Lydia Petrovna and a few puny young birches that grew by her house.

Lydia's Grove was different from the neighborhood where we lived. There, between the sparse buildings there was a vast, empty space, covered with blindingly white snow in the winter months. Gusts of wind came out of nowhere and pinned you down to the ground. I held my mother's sleeve tight and never opened my mouth; the cold air made my teeth ache when I spoke. The schools in Lydia's Grove looked just like ours, as did the supermarkets, wilted trees, and Party slogans. But the houses looked different. They were built like sixteen-story-high narrow boxes, painted white with bright-blue window frames and balconies. A small, old church peeped humbly from between the houses. White plaster had crumbled from its walls, exposing uneven bricks, and ornamental crosses were sawed off, but its golden cupolas still shone brightly in the sun. The inside of the church was used for vegetable storage. A stout, red-faced woman often stood outside sell-ing rotten potatoes and onions. She wore a black quilted jacket with flocks of gray cotton wool sticking out from the torn fabric, felt boots, thick knitted mittens, and a damp apron. She tapped one foot against the other and yelled at her customers: "Don't pick, smartass!" The trampled-down snow around the church was always covered with shiny onion peels.

We passed the church and dived into the lobby of Lydia Petrovna's building, one of the blue-and-white boxes. The lobby was brightly lit and smelled of plaster, paint, and fresh newspapers. On the fourteenth floor, we navigated through the labyrinth of a white hall with identical black doors. My heart began pounding as soon my mother pressed the doorbell, as if I was about to enter a fairy-tale castle and turn into a fairy-tale princess, if only for a couple of hours. The fairy tale started for me immediately after Lydia Petrovna opened the door, with the carved wooden coat-rack on which she hung our coats instead of putting them onto the usual plastic hangers in a closet.

Then she and my mother went into the back room, which was crammed with books, stacks of manuscripts, and loose papers everywhere. I could see them through the open door sitting on an old sofa upholstered in shabby blue velvet. Lydia Petrovna usually wore dark pants and soft, loose white blouses, often with her big opal brooch. I glanced at her and then gazed at my reflection in the mir-ror, trying to imagine myself wearing a blouse like this, instead of a brown acrylic sweater. I smiled at my imagined reflection and made a curtsy.

At times, I watched them working. Lydia Petrovna read the pages in her deep, quiet voice, stopping occasionally to point out something. My mother nodded and made revisions. Sometimes, when she was busy writing, Lydia Petrovna stared at her with a weird, unnerving expression. I thought that she was jealous of my mother's beauty, and I felt sorry for her. Lydia Petrovna wasn't beautiful. She wasn't just plain or homely—she was ugly, with her long fleshy nose and a big wart above her mouth. But when I got used to her ugliness, her face began to seem pleasant. Her gray hair, cut in a bob, was curly like fleece, her small dark eyes were very bright, and she had a beautiful smile. I wouldn't even call it a smile. Her mouth didn't stretch, but her brightened eyes sent a warm glow over her face, making even her wart look nice, like a pink berry that had stuck to her face and had not quite made it to her mouth. She never smiled broadly and never cried, not even at her mother's funeral. She had sat then with a scary, dead expression in her dry eyes while my mother stroked her back and wept.

While we were at Lydia Petrovna's, the front room belonged to me. Once, when it was drafty in the back room, Lydia Petrovna asked, "Larochka, can we work in your room today?" I nodded, blushing from pleasure.

"My room" was large and dim. There wasn't much furniture and no shiny, sparkling, or glossy objects. Instead of the typical crystal vases found in a Moscow apartment, there were bronze statuettes; instead of pictures in glass cases, oil paintings hung in the chipped bronzed frames. Instead of the usual polished wardrobes and stands, there was an old dark-wood desk covered with green cloth and a carved mahogany bookcase. The light coming from the large window was softly absorbed, caressing you instead of blinding you.

I was allowed to sit in the tall chair upholstered with dark, creased leather and draw with the ink pen that used to belong to Lydia Petrovna's grandfather. The long, slightly rusty ink pen, with its wooden handle, was tricky. It either scratched the sheet of paper in vain or made fat blots, but after a few takes I usually managed to write my name and even make a pretty flourish out of the last *a*. I was also allowed to take any book I chose from the massive mahogany bookcase with stubby legs and oak leaves carved on the doors, but I preferred just to look at the leather-bound volumes and stroke them with my finger. When I took a book out, it felt very heavy in my hands. The fragile pages were yellowed and dry. They smelled of stale cookies, and I was afraid that they might crumble in my fingers the way stale cookies can. Most of the time, I simply wandered around the room, devouring every detail. Even after being in Lydia Petrovna's apartment many times, I still found something new and surprising. For example, I never noticed that the bronze Don Quixote on the desk could shake his helmeted head until I touched it accidentally with the ink pen. Or once when I traced my finger over long scratches on the bookcase's surface, I discovered the word "cat" scribbled on the side in big crooked letters. Lydia Petrovna must have done it when she was a child.

After Lydia Petrovna and my mother finished with the manuscript, we went into the kitchen to have lunch. Lydia Petrovna walked briskly ahead of us. My mother followed her, stretching and rubbing her tired eyes. And I had to restrain myself from running to the kitchen.

Unlike the rest of the apartment, the kitchen looked just like any Moscow kitchen: walls painted grayish-yellow, white Formica cabinets, folding Formica table, beige linoleum with a boring pattern, droning refrigerator and enameled kettle on the stove. We sat down on white stools with hard, slippery seats and waited for the table to go through a magical transformation. First the white tablecloth appeared, covering the scratched and chipped surface of the table the way first snow covers the imperfections of the ground; then the cups appeared, light blue with golden rims, made of the finest porcelain; then a cobalt-blue teapot with a silver tea-strainer hooked over its tiny spout. After that, I started fidgeting impatiently on my stool, and Lydia Petrovna put the food on the table at last. We never knew what Lydia Petrovna would serve. It was always something new, something that I'd never tasted before. Afterward, I couldn't remember what food I had eaten—everything had a weird foreign name—but I remembered the sensation of something soft and gentle melting in my mouth with a bouquet of unknown, subtle flavors. Lydia Petrovna didn't cook it—she considered the time invested in cooking a waste. She bought the food in a small deli, hidden on one of the crooked, narrow streets in the old center of Moscow.

During the tea, my mother and Lydia Petrovna usually chatted about their mutual friends in the publishing world. I amused myself by looking through my cup, which was so thin that I could see the silhouettes of my fingers on the other side. I also loved to watch Lydia Petrovna's hands. They were small and pale, with smooth skin and long, narrow fingers. When she spoke, her hands made light, delicate movements in the air, as if they were dancing. From time to time, her dancing fingers moved closer to my mother's hands. My mother reacted in a strange way. She dropped her hands under the table and became tense. I also noticed that my mother never touched Lydia Petrovna even accidentally since a strange mishap they'd had some months before. I was playing in the front room as always, but the door to the back room for some reason was closed. I heard their muffled voices, then the door swung open, and my mother darted out, blushing and agitated. Lydia Petrovna followed her, with her head down. Without saying a word, my mother handed me my coat and began putting on hers. Lydia Petrovna stood leaning on the rickety coatrack with her mouth twitching. Suddenly, my mother turned to her and took her hand. "Lydochka," she said—I was amazed, because my mother never used affectionate names, she never called me "Larochka," only "Lara"— "Lydochka, you'll always be my best friend." It was the last time my mother touched Lydia Petrovna.

I loved it when, during lunch, Lydia Petrovna told stories about her childhood, about her parents, about her parents' twelve-room apartment that didn't seem big enough. "It was before the revolution," my mother explained to me later.

On the train on our way back, my mother told me more stories about Lydia Petrovna. Trying to outshout the subway rumble, she leaned very close to me, tickling my ear with her breath, which made her words even more exciting. "Did you know that their family genealogy can be traced centuries back? Did you know that they are related to Russian tsars, and her great-grandfather was a French diplomat?" I listened with my mouth open. I could trace my own genealogy only as far back as my great-grandmother Clara, and her name was all I knew about her. When we were told in kindergarten that people were descended from monkeys, I naturally assumed that Clara was a monkey. I even drew a monkey on a tree and named the picture *My Great-Grandmother Clara*.

IN JANUARY, we didn't go to Lydia's Grove for three weeks. Lydia Petrovna called to say that she had a cold, then that a distant relation was visiting, then that she had an urgent assignment to write an article.

When we came to Lydia's Grove at last, I could feel that something was wrong. Lydia Petrovna led my mother into the kitchen instead of the back room, explaining that the back room was very messy. They finished their work faster than usual, and during lunch Lydia Petrovna was nervous and distracted and even spilled some milk on the table. My mother rushed to wipe it, and as she was standing with a dishrag in her hands, a woman emerged from the back room and passed us on her way to the bathroom. A tall, skinny woman with a protruding nose and hollow cheeks, wearing purple silk pajamas. The woman glanced at us and said, "Good morning," though it was well past noon. My mother was so stunned that she managed to utter "Hello" only after the woman had already disappeared into the bathroom and we heard the sound of running water. Then the woman came out and headed to the back room, complaining of a headache and the weather change. "She's my friend Emma," said Lydia Petrovna. My mother glanced at me quickly but didn't say anything. She'd been wiping her hands with a greasy dishrag the whole time.

After that, our visits to Lydia's Grove were different. Even though we didn't see much of Emma—she was out most of the time, or sleeping in the back room after a migraine attack, or if she was home and not sleeping, she usually ignored us—we could feel her presence everywhere. She peeked into the kitchen from time to time dressed in pajamas, flowery robes, or bright kimonos, complained about her headache, and asked us politely to speak in lower voices. She also peeked into the front room if I dropped something accidentally, but she didn't say anything, only winced and walked away, shuffling in her fancy embroidered slippers and rubbing her temples. The smell of her dark, disturbing perfume remained in the room after she was gone. I could also feel her presence, seeing paper flowers everywhere: on the desk, on shelves, on window-sills. Emma made them herself and arranged them in shiny crystal vases that she must have brought with her.

I wondered how long Emma was going to stay. Friends sometimes stayed at our house too but never for such a long time.

In February, Emma was still there and had even brought her lap dog, Kitty, to live with her. "Emma missed the dog," Lydia Petrovna whispered to my mother. "To tell you the truth, I'm a little awkward with animals, but Kitty never makes trouble." That was true—Kitty couldn't possibly make trouble. She didn't jump, didn't run, didn't bite, she didn't know how to bark—all she did was lie on your lap and stare at your face.

Kitty usually waited for me to sit down; then, clumsily, slowly dragged her fat body up on my lap, digging her tiny claws into my thighs. Then she made herself comfortable and fixed her round glassy eyes on me. Her whole body seemed frozen except for her tiny moist nose, which kept trembling all the time. There was something unnerving about Kitty's expression. I put her down on the floor, and she never resisted, but in a few minutes she was back on my lap again. My skirt became covered with long white dog hairs.

Kitty did the same thing to my mother and Lydia Petro-vna. When we were having tea, she always came into the kitchen. I tried to distract her with some food, but she only sniffed at it, scratched it with her claws, and immediately climbed into somebody's lap. The only person who enjoyed Kitty's attention was Emma. She often picked the dog up and gave her a smacking kiss right on her wet nose.

Every time we came to Lydia's Grove now, I expected to see more changes. It was like playing a game: Find the Differences. And each time, with a sinking feeling, I found them: lace curtains instead of the heavy velvet blinds, ceramic mugs instead of the blue china set, Emma's photos in glass frames everywhere. Lydia Petrovna always approved, even praised Emma's choices, but I doubted her sincerity. "Look at our new acquisition!" Lydia Petrovna said once, leading us into the front room. Next to the desk stood a massive boxlike object made of glossy polished wood with glass doors. The right side was filled with dishes and vases, the left side with books. My mother gasped. Lydia Petrovna touched the glass doors, making them clink: "Very convenient, and much roomier than my old bookcase." I looked around and only then noticed that the old bookcase wasn't there anymore. My favorite old bookcase with fat little legs and the word "cat" scratched on the side was gone! I desperately tried to push my tears back. Then I noticed Lydia Petrovna's expression. Her mouth was stretched into a smile, but her eyes were sad. She wasn't as happy about the new bookcase as she pretended to be. Why did she let Emma do all these things? Was she afraid of her? I knew better than to ask my mother. She got annoyed every time I mentioned Emma and often snapped at me, "You talk too much!"

Another thing that changed was our meals. We were now served bologna sandwiches and store-bought square cookies, which tasted like flour. Emma said that deli food was unhealthy and too expensive. We ate in silence and every sound—the clatter of spoons or rustle of paper wrap—seemed too loud. Lydia Petrovna didn't join us. She stood at the sink now, wearing a stained flowery apron, cleaning dishes or peeling potatoes. When I looked at her delicate fingers covered with black, sticky peel, the story of Cinderella always came to my mind. I thought that somebody should stand up for Lydia Petrovna, to save her from Emma. In my dreams, it was me. Scenes from heroic Soviet movies flashed in my head. I, dressed in creaky leather boots and a frayed leather jacket, burst into the apartment followed by my soldiers. I raise my shiny revolver and fire away. Emma runs away screaming, along with her dog, her paper flowers, and her new glossy bookcase in a wheelbarrow. I especially enjoyed the image of the wheelbarrow creaking under the hideous shiny mass of the hated bookcase.

I knew that in reality I was powerless. The only thing I could do was to step on Kitty's long ugly tail when nobody saw. I did it once. I stepped on it slightly, but Kitty didn't even whimper, only glanced at me, taken aback. Afterward, on the way home, I felt an itchy sensation in my foot, as if I had stepped on something disgusting.

Soon our meals at Lydia Petrovna's place stopped altogether. One day, Emma walked into the kitchen during our lunch, complained of her headache, and said that she wouldn't mind a cup of tea. Lydia Petrovna rushed to pour her some, but Emma gave us a long, meaningful look and said that she'd wait. After that, every time Lydia Petrovna offered us tea, my mother declined, saying that we couldn't stay long. We ate inside the subway, at the Southwest stop. We sat down on the cold marble bench at the cold marble column, and my mother took out our old yellow thermos and a few melted-together pieces of cheese in a paper napkin. People were staring at us and I tried to eat very quickly, choking on the burning-hot bitter tea and not bothering to remove pieces of napkin stuck to the cheese.

At the end of March, we made our last visit to Lydia's Grove. Lydia Petrovna sat in the kitchen with Kitty in her lap. My mother pulled the manuscript pages out of her bag and put them on the table, but Lydia Petrovna didn't even look at them. Her mouth was twitching. Lydia Petrovna put Kitty down on the floor and said in her calm low voice: "I know that she doesn't love me. Nobody ever will. I accepted that." I waited for my mother to say something, anything, but she was silent. She rose from the table, walked to Lydia Petrovna, and hugged her. I don't know how much time passed before Emma walked in. She was dressed in a dark red silk robe and looked groggy from sleep. She gazed at my mother and Lydia Petrovna with torpid eyes, and then, after a few seconds, let out a muffled scream. She slumped on a stool and began gasping for breath, clawing the skin on her chest with her crimson fingernails. I thought that maybe she was dying; I've never seen anyone die before.

Lydia Petrovna rushed to her with a glass of water, but she threw the water on her, and she pushed Kitty away. Then I couldn't see Emma anymore, because my mother grasped my sleeve and dragged me into the hall, where she tugged my hat and coat on me in a hurry, hurting me in the process.

"Will Emma die?" I asked my mother while we stood waiting for the elevator. She didn't answer, her face was very white and her lips were pressed into a narrow, wrinkled line. I kept watching the door, hoping that Lydia Petrovna would come out and say that we didn't have to go. But when the door opened, it was Emma, standing in the doorway with the manuscript pages in her hands. She threw them on the staircase. Some of them dropped with a thump by the door, others flew down the stairs. Emma's robe fell open, and I could see her black nylon bra hanging on her bony chest. Then Lydia Petrovna grabbed Emma's hand and pulled her inside.

I kneeled down on the cold gray linoleum speckled with dried plaster and picked up the pages. My mother was waiting inside the elevator. She shoved the pages into her bag with dust and hairs stuck to them, and when the elevator started down at last, she sighed with relief.

On our way to the train, my mother walked very fast, without saying a word. I had to run alongside, trying to keep pace with her and step over puddles. Tiny streams of dirty water ran everywhere; the trees, the pavement, and the buildings were darkened and wet. Instead of snow, the space between the houses was covered with dirt and wisps of spring grass. The heavy doors of the church were wide open. Two unshaven men in dark caps were unloading heavy sacks of potatoes and onions off a beaten truck. The saleswoman was now wearing an army trench coat and black rubber boots. She coughed all the time, and her voice sounded strained when she yelled, "Don't pick, smartass!" Shiny onion peels swam in the big puddle by her stand.

I turned to look at Lydia Petrovna's building. It stood second in the line of identical buildings with neat rows of curtained windows. I counted the floors to the fourteenth, but couldn't find her window.

We never went to Lydia's Grove again and soon stopped using that name. We referred to the place as "Southwest," like everybody else.

A Question for Vera

THE ROLL on Katya's plate was growing. She could swear that when she'd started eating it forty minutes ago it was smaller. Katya raised her eyes off the plate and looked around. There were only three of them left at the tables, three slow eaters: Vova Libman, Nina Domova, and Katya. Katya's best friend Aziza would have been there too if she hadn't stayed home with the flu.

Other kids had already finished their midday snack and were allowed to play. They played in the same room where they ate—a big square room painted yellow, with a play section on the right side, a dining section on the left, a kitchen in front and a bathroom in the back—a typical Moscow preschool. Katya could hear chattering, crying, laughter, shrieks, and the clatter of toys. She could be playing too if not for the roll. With a sigh, she took another bite. The roll was not only growing; it was also getting harder. Katya now had to bite with much more force. She peeked into her plastic white mug—it was empty. She considered asking the teacher for more milk but decided against it. Maybe it would help her swallow, but then she would have to deal with the roll and the milk too.

Their teacher, Elena Borisovna, was sitting on the windowsill, cleaning her fingernails with a kitchen knife. Her hips, clad in a light-blue skirt, were spread on the windowsill like a big pillow. She was drumming with a heavy heel of her shoe against the wall: "Boom, boom, boom." Elena Ivanovna had long, twisted hairs growing in the middle of her cheek. She wouldn't let anybody leave the table before they finished, even if only a tiny piece was left on a plate.

The possibility of being the last to finish the meal—of being left all alone in the dining area—filled Katya with horror. If Aziza had been there, Katya wouldn't be so nervous. She and Aziza often finished last. They timed their chewing and swallowed carefully so they would complete a meal at the same time. Then they showed their empty plates to the teacher and went off to play together. But today Aziza wasn't here.

Katya craned her neck to peek at Vova's and Nina's plates. Vova, a scrawny little boy with bent red ears, wasn't eating; he was just staring at his untouched roll hopelessly, while his eyes filled with tears. Each day Elena Borisovna said to him, "A boy crying! What a sight!" Katya was happy to be a girl. Girls were allowed to cry, to wear nice ruffled dresses and try on their mothers' jewelry. Vova Libman didn't care if he was a boy or a girl; he cried all the time. He cried, and when he calmed down, he picked his nose and ate his boogers. If Nina Domova finished first, only Katya and Vova would be left sitting at the table, which would be even worse than having to sit alone.

Katya peeked at Nina Domova's plate. Unlike Vova, Nina was a serious competitor. She was eating slowly, but making steady progress, and the piece left on her plate was definitely getting smaller. Nina Domova didn't bite into the roll; she broke off tiny pieces and stuffed them into her mouth. Katya decided to try that technique. It worked. She even managed to eat faster than Nina, because she could chew harder.

Katya swallowed the last piece—the very last piece was somehow easier to swallow—and carried her empty dishes to Elena Borisovna. Elena Borisovna peered at Katya's plate, peered into Katya's cup, scratched her back with the dull side of her kitchen knife, then sighed and said: "Okay, you can go."

Katya went over to the play area and stopped there, unsure of what to do. If Aziza had been there, they would be playing make-believe games with one another. Most often, they pretended to be beautiful princesses like the ones they saw in picture books—beautiful princesses with golden braids streaming to their feet, even though both Katya and Aziza had closely cropped black hair. Usually, when Aziza was sick, Katya would succumb to playing with other kids. But now the other kids had been playing for some time, and everybody was engaged in one game or another. The groups for nursing dolls, baking cakes, and fighting against the Nazis and the tsar's army had already been formed. In the role games like Mothers-Daughters, Sheep and Wolves, and Geese and Wolves, all the roles had been assigned. There was only one girl, Ira Baranova, who was playing by herself, with a one-eyed doll.

Katya liked that doll. She had even thought of a name for her—Vera, because the doll resembled the famous movie star Vera Orlova. The doll had the same brows, arched and thin. Katya liked to talk to the doll when nobody was listening. She took a few steps toward Ira Baranova so they could play with Vera together, but Ira yawned, picked up the doll, and walked away.

Katya went to the toy bin. There weren't many toys left, just some broken cars and odd items of doll clothing. Katya found four or five pencils on the bottom and decided to draw a princess. She kneeled before a low wooden chair, spread a crumpled sheet of paper on the seat, thought for a moment, took a deep breath, and started drawing. She made two straight, thick yellow lines for the princess's braids. When she was younger, she used to start with the princess's eyes. Later she realized that it was much easier to start with the braids. The braids you could connect with a simple half-circle, and that was it—you had a face.

Katya paused, choosing between blue and aquamarine for the princess's eyes. The aquamarine looked prettier. She was moistening the pencil tip with her tongue to make the color brighter when she felt Ira's stare. Ira was walking toward her, carrying Vera upside down by a leg. She walked very close to Katya and said: "You shouldn't touch a pencil with your tongue. It's bad for you." Katya took the pencil out of her mouth. Ira looked over Katya's drawing and said, "We have to talk." Katya got off her knees and put the pencil down. She watched how the pencil rolled to the edge of the chair with a jolly sound, bounced there a few times, and then fell to the floor. She didn't want to go with Ira. "Come on," Ira insisted, jerking the sleeve of Katya's blue flannel dress.

THEY WALKED into the bathroom and faced the row of white ceramic sinks and the row of white kid-sized toilets in dark-blue stalls without doors. On the wall to the right, there were wooden towel hangers, each with a child's name on it. Katya could see her hanger, second from the left. There was her name: KATYA M. And her towel—white with a tiny green bunny in the corner.

Ira Baranova whispered, "I know something about you." Ira was now standing in front of Katya, blocking her view of the sinks and toilets. Ira was big. She was the tallest kid in their class, with a round face, rosy cheeks, and strict gray eyes. Ira claimed that she had read *War and Peace*. Katya had seen *War and Peace* in her mother's bookcase. She knew that it was a very thick book, maybe the thickest book there. Ira Baranova was a recognized authority on life.

"You are a Jewess," Ira said. "I know. I can tell." Katya

stepped back to the wall, feeling the cold tiles against her shoulder blades. "A Jewess? Why?" Katya didn't know what "a Jewess" meant, or "a Jew," or even "Jewish." She'd never heard these words from anybody in her family or on television, but somehow she immediately understood that she didn't want to be it. "I can't be a Jewess!" she said. Ira Baranova sighed. She reached behind Katya's back, where Katya kept her hands, took her by her right hand, and walked her to the mirror.

It was a small, round mirror, hanging on the wall next to the last stall. Katya could see her own reflection and the left side of Ira's mouth and chin. Ira's mouth was opening and closing, revealing her large moist teeth. "Look at your eyes," Ira said. Katya looked. She had brown eyes, the same color as Uncle Felix's and cousin Lev's, but lighter than her mother's and much lighter than her grandmother's. "Your eyes are too big. It's not normal." Katya turned to look at Ira's eyes. She was right; Katya's eyes were twice as big as Ira's. Two big, round saucers. Katya immediately hated them. "Now, look at your nose." Katya looked, but didn't see anything alarming. Her nose wasn't big; it was even smaller than Ira's. But then she saw Ira's finger in the mirror tracing the outline of Katya's nose. "You see, it's pointed down, not up." That was true. Katya desperately tried to lift her chin up, but the tip of her nose still looked down. Katya wanted to reach for her towel and hide her face from Ira behind the dear green bunny.

"Now, look here," Ira said, staring somewhere down. At that moment the door opened and Nina Domova walked in. She trudged to the first stall and began rolling down her tights along with her underpants. Ira looked at Katya meaningfully and pursed her lips. Katya understood. Their conversation was too serious to be overheard. Nina rolled her tights down to the middle of her thighs and sat on the toilet. She moved back and forth, then slid off and stood up—she hadn't pulled her tights down far enough. She rolled them some more until they got stuck on her knees. She sat back on the toilet. "Will she do a small thing or a big thing?" Katya nervously wondered.

She was glancing at Ira Baranova discreetly while they were waiting, but she couldn't read the expression on her face. Katya avoided looking in the mirror for fear of more dreadful discoveries, but she couldn't stop thinking about what Ira had said. "Your eyes are too big. It's not normal." That meant that to be a "Jewess" was to be not normal, just as Katya suspected. She remembered that she had heard a similar word before. Once, when Katya was in a vegetable store with her mother, a saleswoman had yelled at one of the customers: "Stop picking the good ones! Stop your 'Jewish' tricks!" Katya was now sure it meant the same thing as "Jewess." Some people were "Jewesses." They were not normal and they did Jewish tricks.

Katya knew that her friend Aziza was Uzbek. Was Aziza "normal"? Being Uzbek wasn't bad. Aziza had elongated eyes, thick eyelashes, and tinkling jewelry. On Aziza's birthday, they ate rice with their hands. Aziza's father cooked a big pot of pilaf and put it down in the middle of the room. They sat right on the floor. Aziza, Aziza's parents, and her older sisters could eat with their hands very well; they folded their fingers and carried small portions to their mouths, never dropping anything. Katya couldn't eat like that, and Aziza's father allowed her to eat how she liked. Katya took handfuls of rice, brought them very close to her mouth, and sucked the rice in. Aziza's father laughed and patted Katya on the back approvingly. He wore a long striped robe and a funny round velvet hat on top of his head. Aziza's mother and sisters wore bright shimmering dresses and something like pajama bottoms underneath. Being Uzbek was fun. If Katya had to be something "not normal," why couldn't she be an "Uzbekess"?

Nina Domova had finished. She stood holding the flushing cord in her hands and watched the toilet flush. Her tights and underpants were still down, and she had a thick red line shaped like a toilet seat on her bottom. She slowly pulled up her tights and pulled down her dress. She stopped hesitantly by a sink, then decided against washing her hands and walked out of the bathroom.

"You've got skinny legs," Ira said, without wasting any time. Katya looked down at her thin, ribbed tights twisted around her ankles. That morning, Katya's mother had tried to convince her to wear thicker, woolen tights. But Katya had refused, because the woolen tights made her itch. Now she wished she had listened to her mother. She knew that she had skinny legs. Her older brother had said to her many times: "If you walk into my room once more, I will rip your legs out and put in ski poles instead. Nobody would notice the difference!" Katya wasn't afraid, she knew that he wouldn't do that. Having skinny legs never bothered her before, because she didn't know that it was something Jewish.

Katya flinched as Ira touched her face. Ira pushed Katya's hair aside to expose her small, round ears. Katya's heart was pounding—she was waiting to find out that something was terribly wrong with her ears. What would it be? The size, the shape, the color? Were they too pale? Too yellow? Weren't ears supposed to be pink? "Hmm," Ira said, "your ears don't look Jewish." Katya sighed with relief and smiled gratefully at her dear perfect ears. "But the ears are not important," Ira continued. "You are a Jewess all the same."

Katya's lips quivered—she desperately wanted to cry. "Sorry," said Ira, "I thought you should know." No, Katya couldn't let herself cry in front of Ira. She raised her head up so the tears wouldn't fall from her eyes and tried to assume the posture and expression of Vera Orlova playing Catherine the Great in the old movie. "I'll have to ask my mother. I'm sure you're mistaken," Katya said, trying to gather her dignity, and walked out of the bathroom.

KATYA FELT NUMB for the rest of the day. She didn't enjoy the activities that she usually liked—playing counting games, going for a walk, making imprints of her hands in the snow—and she didn't mind the ones that she usually hated (Elena Borisovna's reading to them aloud, cleaning up the playroom, tying her shoelaces before going for a walk). Katya did everything in a daze, eliciting countless frowns from her teacher and even a few yells: "Move!" "Wake up and sing!" "Come back from the dead!"

From time to time, Katya glanced in Ira's direction. Having informed Katya about her identity, Ira had forgotten about her. She sat quietly in the corner, trying to pluck out Vera's (the doll's) remaining eye with child-safe plastic scissors.

Katya had lied to Ira when she said "I'm sure you're mistaken." She wasn't sure. In fact, she suspected that Ira had spoken the truth. Katya still had some hope that her mother would clear this up—her ears were normal, after all—but the chances of that happening were slim, especially since she knew that ears weren't important. Katya thought of the angry saleswoman in the vegetable store. "Stop your Jewish tricks!" Katya suddenly realized that the customer she was yelling at was Katya's mother! It was Katya's mother who tried to select only the good tomatoes and leave the rotten ones. Katya didn't know why this was bad, but apparently it was. Her mother also had big, "not normal" eyes and the pointing-down nose. So did her grandmother. So did her brother. Acting tough wouldn't save him from being a Jew. All of them were Jews and so was Katya.

It was unfair. Katya didn't deserve to be a Jew. She was a nice quiet girl. She listened to her mother, and to her grandmother. Well, she listened to them most of the time. Maybe she couldn't eat fast enough, but she never talked during the quiet hour, never broke toys, and never fought with the other kids. Just once, she had fought with Aziza, but it didn't last more than a few minutes. They had fought over a boy with whom both of them wanted to fall in love. Katya pulled Aziza's hair, and Aziza bit Katya's hand, but then they decided that Aziza would fall in love with another boy, because she liked him better than the first one anyway.

Katya wished that she had given up that boy then and let Aziza have him. Would Aziza want to be her friend once she knew that Katya was a Jewess? What if she didn't? What if from now on Katya would have to play alone? Maybe she would even have to sit at the table alone. It wouldn't matter anymore whether she ate fast or slowly, she would have to be alone all the time.

THE PRESCHOOL DAY was coming to an end. Elena Borisovna was smearing her big lips with bright red lipstick. The kids were sitting on the low benches, untangling their woolen scarves, putting on their coats, fumbling with buttons and hooks. Nina Domova was scrutinizing the toes of her shoes, slowly lifting and turning her feet. The fully clothed Vova Libman was waiting for his mom by the exit door, crying quietly. Ira Baranova was smoothing out the fur collar of her coat. She had abandoned Vera, who lay facedown in the corner between the lockers.

Katya picked Vera up. She saw that Ira had failed at plucking out the doll's remaining eye—it was still there, shiny and calm as always. Katya shook the pieces of dust off Vera's stringy dark curls. "Vera," she said, swallowing her warm, salty tears. "I am Jewish." Vera wasn't impressed or shocked; she continued to stare at Katya with the same untroubled expression. She wasn't sympathetic. Katya wanted to hit the doll. "You know what, Vera?" she said. "There is a very good chance that you are Jewish too." Katya moved Vera closer to her face. "Look at your eyes! Sorry, at your eye. Look how big and round it is. Do you think this is normal? No, it's not." Vera's nose was positioned very close to her forehead, and it was so tiny that it was very hard to say whether it was pointed down or up. Katya had to move on to Vera's ankles. "Look at your ankles, Vera. Do you think they are thick enough? No. Look at the other dolls' ankles. Can't you see how much thicker they are? And your ears!" Katya took a deep breath: "You have the most Jewish ears I've ever seen, Vera!" Vera's expression didn't change. She looked just as calm as she had before. Katya stared at her, puzzled. "Don't you care, Vera?"

The kids were leaving the room one by one, stepping out onto the staircase where their parents picked them up. Katya was the last one in the line. She saw her grandmother in a fur coat and a fluffy woolen shawl, peering from the crowd of other women in coats and shawls. What if Vera, the doll, was right that there wasn't anything bad or special about being Jewish? Katya looked around. There was nobody to answer that question. Nobody at all.

Mistress

THE DERMATOLOGIST had a mistress. For the past few weeks, it had been the main topic of conversation in his white waiting room, decorated with bright dermatology posters and a lonely, lopsided palm in the corner. This afternoon, there were about eight patients, most of them Russians, seated on red patent-leather chairs, because the office was located on Kings Highway, in a Russian area of Brooklyn. The doctor even had a few Russian newspapers, along with dated issues of *Time* and *Sports Illustrated*, in a plastic magazine rack. But nobody was interested in them.

"He took her to Aroba in November. The mistress," Misha's grandmother was confiding in Russian to a gray-haired woman in a blazer, sneakers, and a long skirt. "Aruba," Misha corrected her mentally. He tried to read a book, but the grandmother's excited whisper filled with fat, rich words like "Aroba" or "mistress" kept him from concentrating. Sometimes she attempted to talk to a woman in a gray beret, seated next to Misha. To do that she leaned over him, putting her heavy elbow on his knee for balance. He had to press his opened book to his chest and wait until she was through, trying to hold his face away from her mixed aroma of sweat, valerian root drops and dill. "First he went on vacation with his wife, but the mistress made a scene, and he had to take her too. They are all like that, you know." The gray-haired woman nodded. At some point, other Russian patients moved closer and joined in the chat. "You mean Dr. Levy has a mistress?" "Yes," the gray-haired woman said eagerly. "He even took her to Aroba." And Misha's grandmother looked at her with reproach, because she wanted to be the one to tell about Aruba.

Every second Thursday after school, Misha had to take his grandmother to the dermatologist. He served as an interpreter, because the grandmother didn't speak English. Misha didn't mind these visits—there wasn't much to translate. Dr. Levy, a small, skinny man with dark circles under his eyes, just glanced at the sores on his grandmother's ankles, scribbled something in the chart, and asked: "How's it going?" Grandmother said "Better" in Russian, and Misha translated it into English. Misha didn't mind the eye doctor or the dentist either. He was saved from attending visits to a gynecologist by his mother and grandfather. "A nine-year-old boy has no business in a gynecologist's office," the grandfather said firmly, surprising everybody, because since they had come to America, it was a rarity to hear him argue, to hear him speak at all.

Misha was happy—for some reason he was afraid of pregnant women with their inflated bellies, fat ankles, and wobbly, domineering way of walking. His mother had to take several hours off work to take the grandmother there. She complained about it and looked at Misha and the grandfather with reproach.

Nobody saved Misha from monthly visits to the internal doctor. The doctor let Misha and his grandmother into his sparkling office with cream-colored walls covered with diplomas and walked confidently to his large mahogany desk. He sat there tall and lean, with a thick mane of bluish-white hair, a red face, and very clean white hands, listening patiently to the grandmother's complaints. Unlike other doctors, he never interrupted her. Misha would have preferred that he did. "My problem is . . . ," she would begin with a sigh of anticipation. She prided herself on being able to describe her symptoms with vividness and precision. "You should've been a writer, Mother," Misha's father once said when she described her perspiration as a "heavy shower pouring from under my skin." Misha's mother looked lost. She didn't know if she should smile at the joke or scold her husband for being ironic about her mother. She chose to smile. "No, a doctor," Misha's grandmother corrected, oblivious to his irony. "I would've become a doctor if I hadn't devoted my life to my husband."

While she talked to the internist, Misha usually stared down, following the checkerboard of the beige-and-brown linoleum floor with his eyes, the pattern interrupted in places by furniture legs and his grandmother's feet in wide black sneakers. Her words were loud and clear, emphasized by occasional groans and changes of tone. "I can't have a bowel movement for days, but I have to go to the bathroom every few hours. It usually happens like this. I feel the urge and go to the bathroom immediately. I push very hard, but nothing happens. I come out, but I feel as if a heavy rock is in there inside me, weighing down my bowels. I go in and try again." The grandmother pressed one of her feet hard into the floor when she described the "heavy rock." Misha looked at her thick, dark stockings. She had brought a supply of them from Russia, along with an assortment of wide-striped garters. Misha felt the edge of his patent-leather chair become moist and slippery under his clutched fingers. He also felt that his whole face was blushing all over, especially his ears. He wondered if the doctor noticed how red they were. But he didn't look at Misha; he looked directly at the grandmother with a patient, polite smile.

"Come on," Misha thought, "stop her. There must be other patients waiting." But the doctor didn't move. Maybe he used these minutes to sleep with his eyes open. "When at last it happens, I feel exhausted, as if I had won a battle. My head aches, and I have a heartbeat so severe that I have to take forty drops of valerian root, lie down, and stay like that for at least an hour." When the grandmother was through, she turned to Misha. The doctor turned to him too, keeping the same polite and patient expression on his face. Misha thought about darting out the door, past the receptionist, past the waiting room, onto the street. He thought about rushing out the window, a large clean window with a plastic model of a split human head on a windowsill. He could see himself falling into the grass, then rising to his feet and running away from the office. But he didn't jump. He just sat there, thinking how to avoid mentioning "heavy rock" or the grandmother's sitting in the bathroom. "Um . . . she . . . my grandmother . . . her problem is . . . she has a . . . she often gets a headache and her heart beats very fast." The doctor smiled at Misha approvingly and wrote a prescription with his beautiful, very clean hands. "Tylenol!" his grandmother later complained loudly to the other patients in the waiting room. "Look at these American doctors! I tell him that I am constipated and he gives me Tylenol! Can you believe that?" The Russian patients sympathized eagerly. Misha hid his burning ears behind *The Great Pictorial Guide to the Prehistoric World*. He wished they would switch to the safer subject of the dermatologist's mistress.

Once they saw her. She flung the door open and walked straight into Dr. Levy's office, not smiling, staring ahead. She was a stout woman in her late thirties, with short reddish-brown hair, in tight white jeans and a shiny leather jacket. She was clomping her high-heeled boots and jingling her gold bracelets as she walked, swinging her car keys in her hand. Everybody in the room stopped talking and followed her with their eyes, even Misha. She had a beautiful mouth, painted bright red. "Shameless!" somebody hissed in Russian. Maybe it was Misha's grandmother.

. . .

AT HOME, Misha did his homework in their long white kitchen, because in his mother's opinion this was the only place that had proper light for him to work and wasn't too drafty. For about a year, the four of them—he, his mother, his grandfather, and his grandmother—had been living in this one-bedroom apartment with unevenly painted walls, faded brown carpet, and secondhand furniture. Everything in the apartment seemed to belong to somebody else. Misha and his mother slept in the bedroom, Misha on a folding bed. The grandmother and grandfather slept on the sofa bed in the living room. Or rather it was the grandmother who slept, snoring softly. The grandfather seemed to be awake all night. Whenever Misha woke up, he heard the old man tossing and groaning or pacing heavily on the creaky kitchen floor.

In Russia, they'd had separate apartments. They even lived in different cities. His grandparents lived in the south of Russia, in a small town overgrown with apple and peach trees. Misha and his parents lived in Moscow. Then his father left to live with another woman. In Moscow, Misha had his own room, a very small one, not bigger than six square meters, where the wallpaper was patterned with tiny sailboats. Misha had his own bed and his own desk with a lamp shaped like a crocodile. His books were shelved neatly above the desk, and his toys were kept in two plywood boxes beside his bed. When his parents argued, they used to say, "Misha, go to your room!" But during the last months before his father left, they didn't have time to send him to his room. They argued almost constantly: they started suddenly, without any warning, in the middle of a matter-of-fact conversation, during dinner, or while playing chess, or while watching TV, and stopped after Misha had gone to bed, or maybe they didn't stop at all. Misha went to his room himself. He sat on a little woven rug between his bed and his desk, playing with his building blocks and listening to the muffled sounds of his parents yelling. He played very quietly.

Misha liked doing his homework, although he would never have admitted that. He laid out his glossy American textbooks so that they took up nearly the entire surface of the table. He loved coloring maps, drawing diagrams, solving math problems: he even loved spelling exercises—he was pleased with the sight of his handwriting, the sight of the firm, clear, rounded letters. Most of all, he loved that during homework time nobody bothered him. "Shh! Michael's studying," everybody said. Even his grandmother, who usually cooked dinner while Misha was studying, was silent, or almost silent—she quietly hummed a theme from a Mexican soap opera that she watched every day on the Spanish channel. Her Spanish was not much better than her English, but she said that in Mexican shows you didn't need words to understand what was going on. The other thing she loved to watch on TV was the weather reports, where you didn't need words either: a picture of the sun meant a good day, raindrops meant drizzle, rows of raindrops meant heavy rain. Misha's mother was against subscribing to a Russian TV channel, because she thought it would prevent them from adjusting to American life. For the same reason, she insisted that everybody call Misha "Michael." Misha's mother was well adjusted. She watched the news on TV, rented American movies, and read American newspapers. She worked in Manhattan and wore the same clothes to work that Misha had seen in the magazines in the waiting room, but her skirts were longer and the heels of her shoes weren't as high.

The problem with the homework was that it took Misha only about forty minutes. He tried to prolong it as much as he could. He did all the extra math problems from the section called "You Might Try It." He brought his own book and read it, pretending that it was an English assignment. He stopped from time to time as if he had a problem and had to think it over, but in truth he just sat there, watching his grandmother cook.

She took all these funny packages, string bags, plastic bags, paper bags, bowls, and wrapped plates out of the refrigerator and put them on the counter, never forgetting to sniff at each of them first. Then she opened the oven with a loud screech, gasping and saying, "Sorry, Michael," took out saucepans and skillets, put them on the stove, filled some of them with water and greased others with chicken fat (she always kept some chicken fat handy, not trusting oil). While the saucepans and skillets gurgled and hissed on the stove, the grandmother washed and chopped the contents of packages and bowls, using two wooden boards—one for meat, the other for everything else. Misha always marveled at how fast her short and swollen fingers moved. In a matter of seconds, handfuls of colorful cubes disappeared in the saucepans and skillets under chipped enameled lids. "I was wise," the grandmother often said to her waiting-room friends. "I brought all the lids here. In America, it's impossible to find a lid that fits." The women agreed, something was definitely wrong with American lids.

To make ground meat, the grandmother used a hand-operated metal meat-grinder, also transported from Russia. She had to summon the grandfather into the kitchen, because the grinder was too heavy. She couldn't turn the handle herself; she couldn't even lift it. The grandfather put his newspaper down and came in obediently, shuffling his slippered feet as he walked, with the same tired, resigned expression that he had worn when he followed the grandmother home from the Russian food store, carrying bulging bags printed with a stretched red THANK YOU. He took off his dark checkered shirt and put it on the chair. (The grandmother insisted that he do that. "You don't want pieces of raw meat all over your shirt!") He put an enameled bowl of meat cubes in front of him and secured the grinder on the windowsill. He stood leaning over it, dressed in a white undershirt and dark woolen trousers. He had brought to America five good suits that he used to wear to work in Russia. Now he wore the trousers at home and the jackets hung in a closet with mothballs in their pockets. The grandfather took hold of the rusty meat-grinder handle and turned it slowly, with effort at first, then faster and faster. His flabby pale shoulders were shaking and tiny beads of sweat came out on his puffy cheeks, his long

rounded nose, and his shiny head. The grandmother sometimes tore herself away from her cooking to offer comments: "What have you got, crooked fingers?" or "Here, you
dropped a piece again" or "I hope I will have this meat
ground by next year." She had never talked to him like that
in Russia. In Russia, when he came home from work, she
rushed to serve him dinner and put two spoonfuls of sour
cream into his shchi herself. The grandfather slurped the
soup loudly and talked a lot during dinner. Now he didn't
even answer the grandmother back. He just stood there,
clutching the meat-grinder handle with yellowed knuckles,
turning it even faster, which made his face redden and the
blue twisted veins on his neck bulge. His stare was focused
on something far away, out the window. Misha thought
that maybe he wanted to jump, like Misha had wanted to
in the doctor's office. But their apartment was on the
sixth floor.

While the food was cooking, the grandmother went to
get her special ingredient, dill. She kept darkened, slightly
wilted bunches spread out on an old newspaper on the
windowsill. She took one and crushed it into a little bowl
with her fingers, to add it to every dish she cooked. At dinner, everything had the taste of dill: soup, potatoes, meat
stew, salad. In fact, dinner hardly tasted like anything else
but dill—the grandmother didn't trust spices; she put very
little salt in their food and no pepper at all. Misha watched
how she moved from one saucepan to another, dressed in a
square-shaped dark cotton dress, drying her moist red face
and her closely cropped gray hair with a piece of cloth,

sweeping potato peels off the counter, groaning when one fell to the floor and she had to pick it up. He couldn't understand why she put so much work into the preparation of this food, which was consumed in twenty minutes, in silence, and didn't even taste good.

Misha couldn't pretend to be busy with his homework forever. Eventually, the grandmother knew that he was done. She watched a weather report on TV and if nothing indicated a natural disaster sent Misha to a playground with his grandfather. "Go, go," she would yell at the grandfather, who sat on the sofa in his unbuttoned checkered shirt, buried in a Russian newspaper. "Go, walk with the boy, make yourself useful for a change!" And the grandfather would stand up, groaning, go to the bathroom mirror to check if he should shave, and usually decide against it. Then he would button his shirt, tuck it into his trousers, and say gloomily: "Let's go, Michael." Misha knew that after they left, the grandmother would take over the Russian newspaper. She would put her glasses on (she had two pairs, both made from cheap plastic, one light blue, the other pink), and slump on the sofa, making the springs creak. She would sit there with her feet planted far apart and read the classifieds section, the singles ads. She would circle some with a red marker she had borrowed from Misha, to show them later to Misha's mother, who would laugh at first, then get irritated, then get upset and yell at the grandmother.

All the way to the playground, while they passed red brick apartment buildings and rows of private houses with little boys in yarmulkes and little girls in long flowery dresses playing on the sidewalks, Misha's grandfather walked a few steps ahead, with his hands folded against his back, staring down at his feet, never saying a word.

Back in Russia, it was different, maybe because Misha was younger then. When he spent summers at his grandparents' place, the grandfather took him to a park willingly, without being asked. He talked a lot while they strolled along the paths of a dark, dense forest: about trees, animals, about how fascinating even the most ordinary things that surround us could be. Little Misha didn't try to grasp the meaning of his words. They just reached him along with other noises: the rustle of a tree, a bird's squawk, a nasty scrape of gravel as he ran his sandal-clad toes through it. It was the sound of the grandfather's voice that was important to him. They walked slowly, Misha's little hand lying securely in the grandfather's big sweaty one. From time to time, Misha had to release his hand and wipe it against his pants, but then he hurried to take the grandfather's hand again.

Now, once they reached the playground and stepped on its black spongy floor, the grandfather said, "Okay, go play, Michael." Then he strolled around the place, searching for Russian newspapers left behind on the benches. He usually found two or three. He walked to a big flat tree stump, in the farthest corner from the domino tables where a heated crowd of old Russian men gathered, and where old Russian women sat on benches discussing their own ailments and other people's mistresses. There, for the full hour that they spent in the playground, the grandfather sat unmoving, except to turn the newspaper pages. Misha didn't know how he was supposed to play. Three-year-olds on their tricycles rode all over the soft black surface of the playground. The slide was occupied by shrieking six-year-olds, and the swings were filled with little babies rocked by their mothers, or with fat teenage girls who had to squeeze their bottoms tightly to fit between the chains. Misha usually walked to the tallest slide, stepping over dabs of chewing gum and pools of melted ice cream. He climbed up to the very top and crawled into a plastic hut. There he sat huddled on a low plastic bench. Sometimes he brought a book with him. He liked thick, serious books about ancient civilizations, archaeological expeditions, and animals who'd become extinct millions of years ago. But most of the time, it was too noisy to read. Then Misha simply stared down at the playground that seemed to move and stir like a big restless animal, and at his immobile grandfather.

THE NOTICE ABOUT the English class was printed in bold black letters on pink neon paper. The color was so bright that it arrested everyone's gaze no matter where it was lying. Since the beginning of March, it could be seen lying anywhere in the apartment: on the kitchen table, in the bedroom on a crumpled pillow, on the toilet floor between a broom and a Macy's catalog, stuffed under the sofa (the grandmother pulled it out from there, blew the pellets of dust off it, smoothed it with her hands, and scolded the grandfather angrily). Everybody studied it, read it, or at least looked at it. They were discussing whether the grandfather should go. He fit the description perfectly. Any legal immigrant who had lived in the country less than two years and possessed basic knowledge of English was invited to attend a three-month-long class on American conversation. "Rich in Idioms" was printed in letters bigger than the rest. "Free of Charge," in even bigger letters. "It's an excellent program, Father!" Misha's mother raved at dinner, removing the bones from the catfish stew on her plate. "Taught by American teachers, real teachers, native speakers! Not by Russian old ladies, who confuse all the tenses and claim that it's classic British grammar." At first, the grandfather tried to ignore her. But Misha's mother was persistent. "You're rotting alive, Father! Think how wonderful it would be if you had something to do, something to look forward to." Misha's grandmother clattered dishes, moved chairs with a screech, and often interrupted this conversation with questions like "Where are the matches? I just put them right here" or "Do you think this fish is overcooked?" She was offended that nobody suggested that she go to the class, even though she knew that the words "basic knowledge of English" hardly applied to her. The best she could do was spell her first name. The last name required Misha's help. But Misha's mother couldn't be distracted by the grandmother's questions or the clattering of dishes. "You'll begin to speak in no time, Father. You know grammar, you have vocabulary, you just need a push." The grandfather only bent his neck lower and sipped his tea, muttering that it was all nonsense and that in their area of Brooklyn you hardly ever needed English. "What about yours and mother's appointments?! Michael and I are tired of taking you there all the time. Right, Michael?" As she said this, Misha's mother moved their large porcelain teapot, preventing her from seeing Misha's face across the table. Misha nodded. It was decided that the grandfather would go.

On the first day of class, the grandfather took one of his jackets from a hanger and put it on, on top of his usual checkered shirt. He asked Misha if he had a spare notebook. Misha gave him a notebook with a marble cover, a sharp pencil, and a ballpoint pen. The grandfather put it all in a plastic THANK YOU bag. In the hall, he took the box with his Russian leather shoes from the top shelf of the closet and asked Misha if they needed shining. Misha did not know, and the grandfather shoved the box back and put his sneakers on. He shuffled out to the elevator, holding the THANK YOU bag under his arm.

From then on, two nights a week—the class was held on Mondays and Wednesdays—they had dinner without the grandfather. His absence didn't make much difference, except maybe that Misha's mother and the grandmother bickered a little more. It usually started with a clipping from a Russian newspaper, a big colorful ad—COME TO OUR PARTY AND MEET YOUR DESTINY. PRICE: FIFTY DOLLARS (FOOD AND DRINK INCLUDED)—and ended with Misha's mother yelling: "Why do you want to marry me off? So you can drive the next one away?" and the grandmother reaching for a bottle of valerian root drops. "I never said a bad word to your husband," the grandmother said plaintively. "You said plenty of your words to me. Didn't spare money in long-distance calls!" "I only wanted to open your eyes!" Then Misha's mother rushed out of the kitchen, and the grandmother yelled after her, carefully counting the drops into her teacup: "How can you be so ungrateful! I came to America to help you. I left everything and came here for your sake!"

Misha's mother had come to America for Misha's sake. She said it to him once, after she got back from a parent-teacher conference. She returned home and said, "Come with me to the bedroom, Michael." He went, feeling his hands grow sweaty and his ears turn red, although he knew that he hadn't done anything bad at school. His mother sat on the edge of the bed and removed her high-heeled shoes, then pulled off her pantyhose. "The teacher says you don't talk, Michael. You don't talk at all. Not in class, not during the recess." She was rubbing her pale feet with small, crooked toes. "Your English is fine, you have excellent marks on your tests. You have excellent marks in every sub-ject. Yet you're not going to make it to the top of the class!" She left her feet alone and began to cry, her black eye makeup running around her eyes. She said to him, snif-fling, that he—his future—was the only reason she came to America. Then she went into the bathroom to wash her face, leaving her rolled-up pantyhose on the floor—two soft, dark circles joined together. From the bathroom, she yelled to him: "Why don't you talk, Michael?"

It wasn't true that he didn't talk at all. When asked a question, he gave an accurate answer, but he tried to make it as brief as possible. He never volunteered to talk. He registered everything that was said in class; he made comments and counterarguments in his head; he even made jokes. But something prevented these already-formed words from coming out of his mouth. He felt the same way when his father called on Saturdays. Misha spent a whole week preparing for his call; he had thousands of things to tell him. In his head, he related everything that had happened to him at school; he described his classmates, his teachers. He wanted to talk about things he had read in books, about lost cities, volcanoes, and weird animals. In his head, Misha even laughed, imagining how he would tell his father all the funny stories he read about dinosaurs, and how his father would laugh with him. But when his father called, Misha went numb. He answered questions but never volunteered to speak and never asked anything himself. He sat with the phone on his bed, facing the wall and picking at old layers of paint with his fingernail. He could hear his father's impatient, disappointed breathing on the other end of the line. Misha thought that his reluctance to talk might explain why his father had not called in several weeks.

NOW THE GRANDFATHER had to do his homework too. Misha came home from school and found him sitting at the kitchen table in Misha's usual place with his notebooks and dictionaries spread across the table. The grandfather would even cut himself little colorful cards out of construction paper and copy down difficult words from the dictionary: an English word on one side, the Russian meaning on the other. He studied seriously and couldn't be bothered during that time. The grandmother had to go to the Russian food store alone, and she brought back smaller, lighter bags because she couldn't carry heavy things. Nobody used the meat-grinder now. It was stored in a cupboard along with other useless things brought from Russia: baking sheets, funny-shaped molds, a small, dented samovar, a gadget for removing sour cherrystones. The grandmother wasn't happy about this. She muttered that she had the whole household on her shoulders and threw looks of reproach at her husband. Misha's mother said: "Please leave him alone—Father has to learn something. It's only for three months anyway." Misha wondered if the grandfather enjoyed his homework as much as he did. He also wondered if the grandfather cheated like he did, pretending that his homework took much more time than it really did.

About three weeks after the class started, the grandfather made up his mind and took the box with his leather shoes down from the shelf. He went to a shoe store and bought a small bottle of dark brown shoe polish. To do that, he had to look up the English term for "shoe polish" in the dictionary. Before each class, he polished his shoes zealously with a piece of cloth. "I don't want the teacher to think that Russians are pigs," he mumbled in response to the grandmother's stare. He squatted with his head down, and his face and neck became very red, as red as they were when he said that he wasn't making enough progress and had to come for extra lessons on Saturdays. The grandmother was putting things away in a cupboard when he said that. She shut the white cupboard door with a satisfied boom. "All that studying and you are not making progress!" One evening the grandfather got up from the sofa, put on his jacket, put some money in the pocket, walked to Kings Highway, and came back with a new shirt, a light-blue one with dark-blue stripes. "It was on sale," he explained to the grandmother.

"'It was on sale!' was all he said to me," Misha's grandmother announced in the dermatologist's waiting room. "If I didn't know him, I would have thought *he* had a mistress." Her listeners, two Russian women, one wearing a thick knitted beret of a lustrous purple color and the other a plain black one, nodded to her sympathetically. "But I do know him." The grandmother grinned and raised one brow to emphasize her words. She looked meaningfully at the women, leaned closer to them, and whispered something. "That—for several years now," she added. The woman in a purple beret said: "But this is good, this is better." The grandmother considered her words and said: "Yes, yes, this is better, of course."

Misha imagined his grandfather with a mistress, with the dermatologist's mistress, because she was the only mistress he'd seen. He imagined his grandfather strolling with her along the Sheepshead Bay embankment with other couples, one of her hands sticking out of the shiny leather sleeve holding his grandfather's hand, her other hand

swinging car keys. Then he imagined her kissing the grandfather on the cheek and leaving a mark with her bright
red lipstick. The grandfather would wrinkle his nose and
rush to wipe it off, the way Misha always did when his
mother kissed him after work. The image of his serious
grandfather rubbing his cheek vigorously made Misha
smile.

Sheepshead Bay was the place where the grandfather
took Misha for his evening walks now. For a few weeks after
the class began, they continued to go to the playground, but
the Russian newspapers were abandoned. The grandfather
took his colorful word cards with him instead. He spread
them on the stump, securing each with a small stone to
prevent the wind from scattering them. Sometimes he read
the words slowly, in whispers, or with his lips moving or
with his eyes. But more often he just looked around with an
incredulous expression as if he were seeing all this for the
first time. Then one day the grandfather said that he was
going to take Michael to Sheepshead Bay to look at the
ships and breathe the fresh ocean air. The grandmother
protested at first, saying that it was a long walk, and it was
windy there, and the boy might catch cold. But the grandfather was firm, almost as firm as he used to be back in Russia. He said that the boy needed exercise and that was that.

On Sheepshead Bay, they didn't stop to look at the
ships. They crossed the creaky wooden bridge and pro-
ceeded along the embankment, passing fishermen, tall
trees, and chipped green benches occupied by lonely-
looking women. At the end of the path, they turned back

and repeated their route three or four times. The grandfather walked ahead, maybe a little faster than usual, limping slightly in his stiff leather shoes. He stared ahead, sometimes turning to look in the direction of the trees and benches. A few times, Misha had the impression that the grandfather nodded to somebody on one bench. Once he slipped on a fish head on the pavement and almost fell while looking in that direction. Misha made frequent stops to look at the fishermen's shiny tackles, the fish heads and tails they used for bait, and the insides of their white plastic buckets, which were usually empty. When the wind was so strong that it chilled Misha's ears and tried to tear his little Yankees cap off his head, there were sharp, dark waves in the water, and Misha could see fish jumping with big splashes. He watched as somebody pulled out his fishing rod, following it with his eyes, holding his breath and licking his lips. He hoped to see a fish being caught at least once. When the grandfather's class was over, Misha was sure that they wouldn't come here anymore. He would have to go back to the plastic hut on the playground, which would get hot in summer and smell of burnt rubber.

THE GRANDMOTHER HAD all her appointments written down on a big wall calendar. It hung next to the refrigerator, a bright spot on a pale kitchen wall. It was called "Famous Russian Monasteries," printed in Germany and sold on Brighton Beach. Below the beautiful, glossy picture of the Zagorsk Monastery, with golden cupolas floating in the brilliantly blue sky, was the schedule for June. The fifteenth, the date when the grandfather's class would end, was circled with Misha's red marker. "See, you didn't want to go, but when it's over you will miss it, Father," Misha's mother said when she passed the calendar on her way to dump her plate in the sink. The grandfather only shrugged. He didn't look moved in any way by her words. It was the grandmother who looked moved, even animated, every time June 15 was mentioned. The great things were to be done then. The grandmother spoke about the ten pounds of cucumbers she wanted the grandfather to bring for her from Brighton Beach. "They are twenty-nine cents per pound there! I will make pickles." She also spoke about the plums and apricots she needed for jam, about sour cherries to make sour cherry dumplings, about little hard pears for marinating, about apples for apple pies. She threw longing looks in the direction of the locked-up meat-grinder, telling about a wonderful recipe she heard in the dentist's office. "I'll make zrazy. Anna Stepanovna says that they come out much better with scallions instead of onions. I'll need a lot of ground beef for them." Then she found a Russian travel agency, which offered discounted tours to elderly people. "We'll go to Boston, to Washington, to Philadelphia. Women in waiting rooms talk about their trips nonstop, and I just sit there too shy to open my mouth. And you will have to go with me," she said to the grandfather. "I won't go alone, as if I weren't married. They put unmarried women on bad seats in the back, next to the toilet." Misha thought that maybe for his grandmother it wasn't such a bad idea to sit next to the toilet, but he didn't say anything. The grandfather didn't say anything either. He only buried himself deeper in his textbook.

ON JUNE 2, a weather report on TV showed a neat gray cloud and dense oblique rows of raindrops. "Heavy showers," the grandmother announced, turning the TV off and walking into the kitchen where Misha and the grandfather were doing their homework, or rather sitting with their textbooks open. "You're staying home tonight." The sky in the window was mostly gray with a few patches of blue. Misha looked further down. People weren't carrying umbrellas, and the gray asphalt of the road was dry and dusty. He looked at his grandfather. The grandfather examined the sky carefully, then lifted the window up a few inches to stick out his arm. The howling gushes of cold wind dashed in, but the arm, although covered with goose bumps, stayed dry. "We'll come back before the rain starts," he said. The grandmother shrugged.

The first raindrops started falling as soon as they left the building. They made dark marks on the pavement but missed Misha and his grandfather. Then a raindrop fell right on the tip of Misha's nose. He wiped it off. Close to Sheepshead Bay, the grandfather stopped and stuck out his open palm. Some drops landed on it. "It's not rain, is it, Michael?" the grandfather asked, turning to Misha and wiping his damp face with his damp palm. Misha shrugged. They both looked in the direction of the bay. It was very close, they could see the ships, and the dirty-gray high waves, and the tops of the trees bending low under the pressure of wind. Newspaper pages, probably left on the benches, were flying up. "It's not a heavy rain. Let's make one round. Okay?" Misha nodded, holding tight to his cap. They crossed the street, the only ones to walk in the direction of the park. Most people hurried out. Big round raindrops were now falling fast, hitting the pavement one after another with a smacking sound and turning small wet spots into intricate ornaments, then into puddles. The grandfather stopped hesitantly and looked in the direction of the benches. There was nobody there. "I think we'd better head home, Michael," the grandfather said. "It's starting to rain."

The heavy downpour reached them while they were waiting for the streetlight to turn to green. With all the wind's howling and the sounds of rain, they didn't immediately hear somebody calling for them. Or rather, Misha heard, but he didn't grasp at once that it was his grandfather's name being called. "Grigory Semyonovich! Grigory Semyonovich!" Nobody had used his surname since they left Russia. A small old woman in a brown raincoat, holding a plastic bag above her head, was running to them, stumbling in black water-resistant boots too wide for her. Misha pulled the grandfather on the sleeve, making him stop and turn. "Grigory Semyonovich! Come to my place, come quickly, the boy will catch cold," she said breathlessly, trying to position her plastic bag above Misha's head.

• • •

HER PLACE WAS ON the top floor of a three-story brown-stone across the street from the park. They walked up a dark staircase that smelled of something unpleasant. "Cats?" thought Misha, who had never smelled a cat. The woman led the way. She was still out of breath and spoke in short, abrupt sentences. "Poor boy. Grigory Semyonovich. How could you. In weather like this. I was there on a bench. But I left. As soon as the rain started. I saw you from across the street. I'm worried about the boy." The grandfather was also out of breath, and silent.

Inside, Misha had only a moment to notice that the apartment was very small and dimly lit before a big rough towel, smelling of unfamiliar soap, covered his face and shoulders and back. He felt the woman's swift little hands rubbing his body. He became ticklish and wanted to sneeze.

"My name is Elena Pavlovna. We go to school together, your grandfather and I," the woman said after Misha and the grandfather had refused dry sweatpants but accepted dry socks and their shoes had been stuffed with newspapers and put to dry in the bathroom. They were drinking hot chocolate at the one-legged round table in the tiny kitchen. Misha's grandfather and Elena Pavlovna had made the hot chocolate together. The grandfather poured boiling water from the kettle, holding it by the wooden handle with both hands. Elena Pavlovna put the mix into three yellow mugs and moved them closer to the kettle. They said "Thank you", "Please," and "Would you" to each other and smiled frequently. They spoke like characters in the Chekhov adaptations that Misha's mother loved to watch in Russia, yet Misha could feel that with his grandfather and Elena Pavlovna it wasn't an act. "What's your name?" Elena Pavlovna asked. "Michael," said Misha. "Michael?! You don't look like a Michael. Misha would suit you better. Can I call you Misha?" Misha nodded, blowing with pleasure on his too-hot drink (at home the grandmother would usually add a bit of cold milk) and biting into a cookie with delicious raspberry jam inside. "Store-bought," Elena Pavlovna said. "I don't bake. Why bother when there are so many delicious things sold in bakeries? Right? But that's not the real reason. I am simply a very bad cook." Misha could see that she wasn't ashamed to admit this.

Her apartment was smaller than theirs. One room and a kitchen. It was furnished just like theirs: a hard brown sofa from a cheap Russian furniture store, a scratched coffee table and a chest of drawers retrieved from the trash, heavy lamps bought at a garage sale. Delicate Russian tea set and books in a dark cabinet with glass doors. Misha read the titles of the same books they had brought from Russia—Chekhov, Pushkin, historical novels with dark, gloomy covers, Maupassant and Flaubert translated into Russian, thick dictionaries, Russian-English and English-Russian. Some titles were obscured by two big photographs. One showed two serious, curly-headed girls, both older than Misha. "My granddaughters," Elena Pavlovna said with a sigh. "They live in California with my son." On the other picture, in black and white, was a smiling young man in a uniform. "Her son," Misha thought, but Elena Pavlovna said that it was her husband.

Elena Pavlovna had a braid, a thin gray braid coiled on the back of her head. Misha had never seen an old woman with a braid before. The hair coming out of the braid framed her face with a crown of fluffy grayish-white curls. Her skin was dry and thin, with neat little wrinkles that looked as though they were drawn on her face with a pencil. Her eyes were small and dark. They misted over as she read them her sister's letter from Leningrad. "Everything is the same: the Neva, the embankment, the Winter Palace; only you, Lenochka, are gone." The grandfather patted her hand when she said that. She wore a blue woolen dress with a high collar covering her neck and a large amber brooch. "Want to look at my brooch, Misha?" she asked, unpinning it. "My mother said that there was a fly inside." Misha held the large, unpolished piece of amber in his hands. It was cool and smooth on top, rough on the edges. There was a strange black mass inside with thin sprouts looking a little like an insect's legs. "I am not sure myself, maybe it's just a crack," Elena Pavlovna said. "Do you know, Misha, what amber is?" "Yes," he answered eagerly, turning the piece of amber in his hands. "It's hardened tree tar; flies could get stuck in it while it was still soft and gluey. Yes, I think it is a fly, only a deformed one." Misha raised his eyes off the brooch and blushed, seeing that both Elena Pavlovna and his grandfather looked pleased with what he said.

Outside, everything was wet and brightened by the

rain. The trees released showers of raindrops on their heads when they passed under them. They walked very fast, close to each other, their wet shoes squishing on the black, wet asphalt. They had left Elena Pavlovna's apartment as soon as the rain ended. Their shoes were still damp, but they took the sodden newspapers out and put the shoes on. Elena Pavlovna didn't protest, didn't say that they must wait, that Misha might catch cold from wearing damp shoes. On the staircase, she took his hand in her dry, small one and said: "Come again, Misha." But Misha doubted that he would ever see her again. He also knew that she wasn't to be mentioned at home. They would probably have to say that they waited until the rain was over in the hallway of some building or inside a deli. Elena Pavlovna, a woman with a gray braid and an amber brooch, would be his and the grandfather's secret. For some reason, Misha felt an urge to take his grandfather's hand, but then he thought that nine-year-old boys don't walk holding their grandfathers' hands. Instead, he began talking about the formation of amber, about volcanoes, about chameleons, about dinosaurs that swallowed big rocks to help them grind their food, about crocodiles that did this too. He talked nonstop, breathlessly, sputtering, chuckling in excitement, interrupting one story to tell the next. He looked at his grandfather, whose eyes were focused on Misha, who nodded in amazement and muttered from time to time: "Imagine!" or "Imagine what living things have to come up with to survive!" And Misha wanted to tell him more, to hear the "Imagine!" again and again. Close to their building, the grandfather suddenly stopped, interrupting a story about comodo dragons. "Misha," he said, sounding a little out of breath. "You know what, my class won't be over on June fifteenth. I mean it will, but I'll find another class, then another. Misha, there are a lot of free English programs in Brooklyn. You have no idea how many!" A big raindrop fell on the grandfather's head from the tree. It ran down his forehead, lingered on his large nose, and hung on the tip. The grandfather shivered and shook his head like a horse. Misha laughed.

Love Lessons—Mondays, 9 A.M.

THE PRINCIPAL, Maria Mikhailovna, was a tall, heavy woman, well over two hundred pounds, with her lower part heavier than her upper. The students nicknamed her "the Pear." When she walked, the heels of her black pumps left deep imprints in the linoleum. Without lifting my eyes, I could see that she was walking toward me. I silently prayed that at the last moment she would change direction.

From my recent experience as a student, I knew that when a principal was approaching you, it was best to keep your eyes down. I wasn't a student anymore, but I sat looking at my knees, which stuck out from under my gray pleated skirt. I hated my knees. They were bony, red, and often scratched or bruised. A little girl's knees, not a teacher's knees.

Twenty-two of us sat along the walls of the teachers' lounge. I was the youngest. In fact, I wasn't even a teacher; I was eighteen years old, only in my second year of college, but the school needed somebody to teach tenth-grade math so desperately that they hired me. The other teachers were all women between the ages of thirty and sixty, except for Sergey, the history teacher, who was twenty-five and male. All the female teachers wore dark skirts and nylon blouses. Most of them styled their hair in old, flattened perms. The young teachers used some mascara and lipstick, while the older ones wore no makeup at all and used the same cheap yellow soap that was supplied in the school bathrooms, making their faces and hands smell distinctly of school.

Maria Mikhailovna read to us from a thin brochure as she marched around the room. She had the deep, loud voice of a person who talked for a living. My mother had the same voice—she had hosted political-awareness sessions in schools and factories for years.

Although Maria Mikhailovna read very well, nobody seemed to listen. Some teachers chatted, others read *Young Muscovite,* a new daily paper that printed only shocking stories, a novelty in Russia. A few days earlier, I'd read an article about a dog that had bitten off her owner's genitals when the owner tried to rape her. And a month earlier about a gang called the Skinners, whose members kidnapped fat people, skinned them alive, and made hamburgers out of them.

Maria Mikhailovna stopped hesitantly next to me, pausing in her reading. She shifted her weight from one foot to the other, sighed, and touched the back of my chair.

I stopped breathing. But then the floorboards creaked and she started walking away. I took a few quick breaths and lifted my eyes. She was definitely walking away from me, tapping the palm of her hand with her brochure.

The brochure was entitled *Sex Education: The Theses*. The Ministry of Education had sent it to every school that year to introduce sex education in the tenth grade. Now the faculty had to pick two sex education teachers. I had good reason to worry. Whenever there was an unpleasant errand or assignment that nobody wanted to do—supervising monthly school dances and weekly yard cleanings, taking students on trips to Lenin's tomb, running out to a bakery to buy a cake for the teachers' tea—Maria Mikhailovna picked me, "our young teacher." She always referred to me as "our young teacher." Her use of the word made "young" sound like a mark of inferiority and inevitable failure. Sometimes she peeped into my room during class, sticking her pink face inside the door and leaving her heavy body outside. She watched me teach for a few minutes, which made me sweat, sputter, confuse words, and drop my chalk on the floor. If one of my students so much as stirred or smiled, she said, "Shame on you! Don't you respect your young teacher?" or "We know she is young and it's very hard for her to handle you, so help her! Show some respect!" I kept my eyes down and dug my fingernails into the flesh of my palms. I wished that the most horrible things would happen to Maria Mikhailovna. I fantasized about her getting caught by the Skinners and turned into a hamburger.

Sergey wasn't very old or experienced either, but Maria Mikhailovna never referred to him as "our young teacher." She called him "our male teacher," with affection and awe, as if his gender were an admirable character trait.

Sergey had naturally just been appointed to teach sex education to the boys. He didn't mind. He seemed to know enough about sex. Every Friday, a different smug girl in nice imported clothes stood waiting for him on the school porch after classes. Every Friday, I watched from my classroom window, half-hidden behind dusty flannel curtains. At three-forty Sergey would appear on the porch, in faded jeans and a dark shirt with the top two buttons undone, carrying a wrinkled jacket and a crumpled pack of cigarettes. From my fourth-story window his back looked a little slouchy. Sergey wasn't very handsome, but it didn't matter to me. He walked up to the girl on the porch, smiled at her, gave her a peck on the cheek, and put his arm around her waist. He looked into the girl's eyes with a promising expression. I let go of the curtains and sighed.

Not that I was in love with Sergey. What I felt for him was nothing compared to what I had felt for Prince Andrey from *War and Peace,* or for the math teacher from my hometown, or for the famous actor Alexey Batalov, who played a fatally ill nuclear physicist in my favorite movie, *Nine Days of One Year.* I wasn't in love with Sergey, but I would have liked it if he looked at me with a promising expression.

Except for me, Sergey was the only one who paid attention to Maria Mikhailovna. He sat leaning forward, with his sharp elbows propped on his knees, light-brown eyes narrowed with attention, waiting for an opportunity to make a fool out of Maria Mikhailovna, which he did all the time. Back in school, he was probably one of those students who were always asking their teacher provoking questions. When Maria Mikhailovna said that our school was proud to have the lowest rate of unplanned pregnancies in Moscow, Sergey asked what the rate was for planned pregnancies. I wouldn't have wanted to have somebody like him in my class. But Maria Mikhailovna didn't mind—she responded to his quips with one of her warm, all-forgiving smiles. She smiled at him even when he didn't say anything.

Maria Mikhailovna finished reading about the disastrous effects of the lack of sex education in Soviet schools, and moved on to a chapter praising countries where sex education was highly developed. When she read, her heavily painted eyelashes blinked, and the tip of her nose moved up and down. "In the United States, *ten-year-olds* know how to use a condom!" Sergey's eyes lit up with excitement. "Ten-year-olds using condoms! I wonder what they put them on."

I dropped my gaze and tried not to giggle, biting my lower lip and digging my nails into my knees. But a little squeal of laughter sputtered out, enough to attract Maria Mikhailovna's attention. "It's easy for you young people to laugh!" When I raised my head, she was looking at me with her famous knowing smile. "You think you know everything and we older people know nothing. Well, the time has come to share your knowledge." She plopped the brochure into my lap and stopped smiling. I saw that she was serious. I also saw that the decision had been made long before this meeting and that I couldn't have done a thing about it. They all stared at me: twenty female teachers with bad perms, one unflinching principal, and one smirking Sergey.

AT HOME, I sat on the edge of the narrow bed where I slept and stared at the brochure. My Aunt Galya had agreed to let me live in the back room of her apartment when I came to study at Moscow University. The room was so small that my feet touched the wardrobe when I sat on the bed.

I had read the brochure twice, but it wouldn't have helped if I'd read it ten times. The authors did a good job of stressing the importance of sex education and had included a detailed list of topics to cover, but there wasn't anything, not a word, not a hint, of what exactly teachers were supposed to say on those topics. On Monday, I would have to walk into the classroom and announce to the tenth-grade girls that I was there to give sex education lessons. Would they laugh, or would there be a deadly silence? Would they ask probing questions? Would they laugh when I tried to answer them? Actually, they'd probably just exchange knowing looks, small smiles, sly winks. If I turned my back to them, I would hear stifled giggles and feel that tickling sensation in my spine that I always felt when I knew they were mimicking me.

I started crying, and a tear dropped onto the open

brochure in my lap. I didn't care if it got soaked. It was useless. I wanted my mother, who was in our little home-town hundreds of miles away from Moscow. But I knew better than to call her. If I did, I would start sobbing right away, and I would drown out her voice crackling through the poor connection. During my last months at home, everything about my mother irritated me: her questions, her suggestions, her endless pestering—even the sound of her voice. I couldn't wait to hop on a Moscow train and leave for my new life. At the station, I didn't even bother to kiss her before I climbed the steps onto the train. Then I saw her standing on the platform scanning the train's dusty windows in search of me. I waved at her quickly and walked away from the window.

I wished I had somebody, anybody, to talk to. I'd been living in Moscow for a little over a year, and I'd lost touch with all of my high-school girlfriends and hadn't made any new ones. Moscow girls seemed too snobbish and too well dressed to try to approach. When I spoke to them, they furrowed their brows, as if I spoke a foreign language and they were struggling to understand me. The girls who, like me, came to the university from small towns all lived on campus. They had immediately formed a close-knit circle bound by their own specific interests. They discussed how to use forbidden electric teakettles, how to dry clothes on rusty radiators and sneak boyfriends into their rooms at night. They exchanged information about dealing with hangovers, flooded toilets, and mean Muscovites. I couldn't be a part of this set. Simply by living with my aunt, I wasn't a part of it. What is more, they considered me a Muscovite precisely because I lived with my aunt.

I saw my distorted reflection in the glossy surface of the wardrobe. I drew my knees up to my chin and moved closer to the wall. Above my head, the photographs of Aunt Galya's late husbands, Uncle Ivan and Uncle Boris, hung slightly off-center on the faded wallpaper. Ivan was in his twenties in the picture, and Boris in his fifties; both men had stubby noses and small, gloomy eyes. They could've been father and son. Every morning, Aunt Galya came into my room, climbed onto the bed, spat on the glass, and wiped the pictures with a dishrag.

I COULD HEAR Aunt Galya moving around in the living room as I wiped away my tears. The dishes tinkled as she shuffled around, humming something out of tune, clearing her throat every now and then—all sly, subtle hints that she wanted my company. The humming and throat clearing would get louder and more persistent, and soon Aunt Galya would appear at my door and ask if I wanted a cup of tea. I would have to come out and try to look enthusiastic. Aunt Galya was a distant relative of my mother. In fact, they'd only seen each other a few times. It had been very generous of her to let me live here. My mother would have gone crazy with worry if I had had to share a dorm room with three other girls—with three "drunken sluts," in her words. And it would have been base ingratitude for me to refuse to sip a cup of tea with Aunt Galya and listen to her stories.

The stories were either about Aunt Galya's dead husbands or about her countless admirers. During that year, I'd learned all their names, addictions, habits, and physical peculiarities. I'd learned, for example, that Uncle Boris had a hairy back, Uncle Ivan had small balls, and Uncle Ivan's best friend Vasiliy had even smaller ones.

Aunt Galya appeared in my doorway almost every night, holding her faded silk robe over her large breasts. Her robe used to be a kimono, but she had cut holes on one side and sewn buttons on the other. She could button it up when she wanted, but she never did. "Come, have a cup of tea with me." But Aunt Galya never served me tea. I doubted if she had tea or a teakettle, or even a pot. Aunt Galya wasn't big on cooking. She usually ate her meals at the factory where she worked. On weekends she had a bologna sandwich for breakfast, a bologna sandwich for lunch, and chocolate candies for dinner. Every time I came out of my room for "a cup of tea," Aunt Galya would put a big glossy box of candies on the table and rush to the kitchen. She came back holding a glass jar filled with a turbid greenish liquid. Moonshine. She made it herself, a fresh batch every Saturday morning, and kept it in glass jars with old faded labels: STRAWBERRY JAM, DILL PICKLES, PICKLED MUSHROOMS, EGGPLANT CAVIAR. She poured moonshine from the jar into her cut-glass tumbler, drank it slowly, ate a candy, and then poured again. She never drank more than half a liter in the course of an evening. She wasn't as strong as she used to be. Although she was fifty-seven, she looked older, and her stomach ulcer had made her complexion sallow. She spent her evenings at home, listening to the radio or simply lying on the couch.

AUNT GALYA'S STEPS stopped. She must have sat down. I heard the unsteady tinkling of the glass jar against the edge of the tumbler. Long, drunken yawns were beginning to replace her humming. That meant that she would be falling asleep soon and I wouldn't have to come out and listen to her. Yet I felt somewhat disappointed, which surprised me. Even listening to her stories would have been better than sitting here alone and mourning my ruined life. I dropped onto my hard bed with a thump and resumed crying, wetting Aunt Galya's pillow this time. I wanted my mother. If not my mother, then at least my own pillow, not this small stiff thing with its silly lace trimming.

ON MONDAY MORNING, I felt better. "Maybe it won't be a disaster," I thought. I walked past the huge gray buildings of Moscow on my way to the school, and the crisp air stung my cheeks as if it were winter already. The trees were stripped of leaves but not yet covered with snow. It made the streets look wider. When I'd first moved to Moscow, the streets had seemed so strange and hostile. But after a few months I grew to like them. Moscow streets were like big rivers: wide, endless, and flowing. Everything—cars, people, autumn leaves—was constantly moving, and I felt swept up in it as I walked fast, my scarf flapping in the wind. I caught my reflection in a supermarket window. Even through its stained, poorly washed glass, I could see that I looked pretty.

The handles of my oversized canvas bag cut into my palms. The bag was weighted down by the book I had checked out from the library over the weekend. It was 980 pages, entitled *The Nature of Sexuality*. It was written by several authors, each one with a Ph.D. next to his name. The book was the only one in the library with the word "sex" in the title. I shifted the bag in my hands. Its heft was reassuring. It also contained a bright folded poster that I had copied the night before from a picture in *The Nature of Sexuality*.

I recalled that before my first math lesson I had been frightened too, but it had turned out all right. Nobody mimicked me or laughed in my face. The students sat quietly leaning over their notebooks, I didn't do anything wrong, and my voice faltered only two or three times. Maybe my sex instruction would be all right too. I had my book and my poster, and it was not as if I had no experience whatsoever. I wasn't a virgin. Or at least I hoped I wasn't. Actually, I couldn't be completely sure about it.

I arrived at school a few minutes earlier than usual, so I had time to secure my poster on the blackboard. I spread it on the table and picked out eight rusty tacks from the drawer. The poster, which I had created by gluing eight regular sheets of paper together, was large. In the center was a colorful drawing of the female reproductive organs with their Latin names shooting out from it like fireworks. Aunt Galya had peeked into my room and asked if I was drawing "chicken innards." It did not look like chicken innards at all! I had gotten the colors right, and I was especially happy with the intense purple of the uterus, a color I created by applying blue paint on top of red. I wasn't as happy with the shapes and sizes though. It proved difficult to make the poster eight times larger than the picture in the book and maintain the right proportions. I could see now that one ovary was larger than the other. But at least the poster was bright and eye-catching. Even intimidating. And that was a good thing.

I usually started my math lessons by writing some difficult equations on the blackboard and demanding that they be solved in ten minutes. I called it "warming up," but my real goal was to intimidate the students. I walked into the classroom, stumbling in my mother's pumps, with parched lips and cold trickles of sweat running down my sides. And they were sitting there, all thirty-nine of them, big, smug, scary. Everything about them was scary: their pimpled foreheads and red fingers, their blue uniforms darkened under their arms, their cracking voices, the boys' enormous feet in scuffed shoes, the girls' awkward makeup. They could eat me alive. Math was my only weapon, because I knew it and they didn't. I followed one assignment with another without a break. I gave them tests every couple of days and assigned excruciating homework. I was very strict about grading papers. They could be sure that not a single mistake would go unnoticed. Needless to say, I never smiled during my lessons. My students called me "the Math Hound" or simply "the Hound" behind my back. I didn't mind that name. They feared me. I had them under control.

The last tack bent back instead of piercing the board. I straightened its tip and punched it in, then massaged my fingers and stepped aside to admire my work. Yes, it looked scary enough. I pulled down the projector's screen to cover the poster until the appropriate time. I was ready.

The girls slowly entered the room, which looked strange with gaps where the boys usually sat. (The boys had been taken to Sergey's classroom across the hall for their class on sexuality.) It was unusually quiet. The girls moved their chairs carefully to avoid making scraping noises, talked in whispers, and exchanged shy looks. "Good morning!" I said. My voice rang out clearly in the silent classroom. Though I always said those words at the beginning of math lessons, I wasn't prepared for the girls' reaction now. Instead of groaning, then sighing, then peering at their homework, they looked up at me with strange, expectant expressions. Could it be interest? I wasn't sure, because I'd never seen my students look interested before. Then something occurred to me, something that would have made me laugh if I hadn't been so nervous. They saw me as their teacher. They thought I possessed certain knowledge of sex the way I possessed certain knowledge of math. But unlike math, sex was something they really wanted to learn.

A girl in the first row was tapping her foot on the ground. Another girl by the window rubbed the pimples on her forehead with the tip of her pen. My best math student, the pretty Sveta Zotova, twisted her ash-gray curls around her finger. Suddenly, these girls didn't seem so big or tall or grown-up to me. They could have been girls like I'd once been, with their mothers telling them, "You'll figure it out, when the time comes." The ground was slipping from under my feet. What if the girls were not my enemy? No, I couldn't let them fool me! I wasn't going to soften up. I would beguile them with my poster, then finish them off with Latin terminology. I unveiled my poster and spoke the sentence that I'd been working on for the last two days: "We'll begin our lessons by studying the organs responsible for sexual functions in the female body."

AUNT GALYA HAD come home early that day and was cooking when I came in. As soon as I opened the front door, I felt waves of heat coming from the kitchen, and the sweetish smell of burnt milk crept into the hall. Apparently, something was gurgling under the lid of the big aluminum pot. I'd never seen this pot before. Aunt Galya must have borrowed it from a neighbor, along with the green apron that was tied over her "kimono." She stood beside the stove with a dishrag in one hand and a wooden spoon in the other. Every few seconds, she raised the lid, let out clouds of white steam, and stirred what was inside. Her face was flushed. "I'm making kasha! Good for your stomach," she announced. "I had another doctor's appointment today, and guess what he said? That I should eat a lot of kasha and drink less!" She poured some salt into the pot from the opening in the two-pound bag, then tossed in a handful of sugar from the sugar canister. She wiped her forehead with the dishrag and turned to me. "Want some?"

Aunt Galya served us both kasha in large golden-rimmed plates with crimson roses painted on them. We ate slowly, working from the outer edges of the plates to the center. Aunt Galya was sober and quiet. I hoped that filling myself with kasha would help me get rid of the gnawing sensation in the pit of my stomach. The kasha was hot, heavy, and gluey. I wanted each next spoonful to dissolve the memory of my sex lesson.

None of my nightmares had been realized. Nobody made fun of me, nobody laughed, nobody even smiled during my lesson. Yet somehow it seemed that what happened was even worse. I kept thinking of Vera Bunina's expression when she asked her question at the end of the hour. Vera, a quiet, overweight, somewhat slow girl, was painfully shy. For her to raise her hand and ask a question, any question, was a big deal, especially since her classmates often laughed when she spoke. She had pointed at my poster with her pale, puffy hand and asked if every woman and every girl had "that," probably wondering whether "that" was actually as huge and ugly as I had drawn it. I expected the girls to laugh. I avoided looking at Vera's homely face, thinking how it would redden and tremble at the burst of laughter. But nobody laughed. The girls sat silently staring at the poster. I wondered if some of them did the same thing that I had done back home. Shivering in our moldy bathroom, I used to put my mother's hand mirror on the floor and squat down, straining my neck to have a look at it. Afterward, I lay in bed crying, feeling frightened and appalled, because it looked so ugly. I had a startling image of myself sitting at one of the desks among the girls, looking at the poster, and feeling even more frightened and appalled.

The tears were starting to cloud and burn my eyes, and a heavy lump was rising in my throat. I tried to push it back down with spoonfuls of kasha. "It is good, isn't it?" Aunt Galya asked, blowing on hers. I nodded.

The girls had silently emptied the room as soon as the bell rang. Then, while I struggled with my rusty tacks—I wanted to take my poster off before my math lesson started—the door across the hall flung open and the boys spilled out of their classroom in groups, all blushing, excited, giggling, some even bursting out in their coarse, neighing laughs. I saw grinning Sergey in the doorway. He stood behind two of his boys, who blocked his way trying to ask him something. He scrunched his face and scratched his forehead, pretending to think hard, then he said something with a very serious expression. The boys laughed. Sergey prodded them to move them from the doorway and walked down the hall with his usual lazy gait.

I scraped kasha remains from the bottom of my plate, exposing crimson roses. I wondered what Sergey talked about in his lesson. I imagined that he shared something from his own experience. That was why the boys felt at ease with him. Then he urged them to ask questions—anything they wanted to know. I wondered if I could do the same? Just talk to the girls about my own experience, honestly, making them feel at ease with me and encouraging them to talk openly about their experiences?

No, I couldn't do that. I took another helping of kasha and began swallowing it rapidly. When I lived at home, I'd only had one unimpressive, even embarrassing, sexual encounter with a boy from my class. I couldn't possibly talk about that. Or about the fact that for the year that I had lived in Moscow nobody had asked me on a date. I tried to tell myself that it wasn't my fault, that I didn't go to parties, that I spent all my time working and studying and preparing for my lessons and my exams. But I did ride the subway and buses, and I did go to the Central Library and to art museums, and I knew that you could meet somebody at those places, but nobody had ever asked me for my phone number.

I was startled by a sudden tinkling sound. "It's time for my medicine," Aunt Galya said, pouring the green liquid from a jar labeled EGGPLANT CAVIAR into her cup. "The doctor said that drinking is bad for me!" Aunt Galya snorted loudly. "Can you believe that? Drinking has been keeping me alive all these years! It's folk medicine. It goes way back." She drained her cup and blinked several times. She did look more alive after a drink. It brought some pink to her cheeks and made her eyes greener and brighter. Glimpses of her former attractiveness came out. I wondered if there was any truth in the stories of her glorious past love life. Often after "tea," Aunt Galya offered to share her love secrets. "Listen hard, I'm gonna teach you how to love!" she would announce while pouring out moonshine. I usually declined, making polite excuses about having to study. At other times, Aunt Galya felt like showing off her body. She would stand up, straighten her back, and say, "Just look at this! Can you see why men are so crazy about me?" I saw an aging woman in a shabby kimono, with a massive upper body, a sagging stomach, bony hips, and pale, skinny calves with twisted hairs along the bone. I saw a blotched face with small eyes the color of moonshine under heavy eyelids. Aunt Galya hardly looked like a sex goddess, especially now, when she sat staring mournfully into her empty teacup. But what if she did know something about sex? What if her love lessons were worth listening to? I had nothing to lose. I gathered up my courage and said: "Aunt Galya . . . Do you mind if I ask you a few questions?" She slowly raised her head, her expression changing from incredulous to questioning to gleeful. She moved her teacup away and ran her hand through her short, wavy hair, preparing to talk. "Aunt Galya, wait!" I rushed to my room for a notebook and pen.

In December, the schoolyard was covered with snow-drifts. The caps of soggy snow lay everywhere: on the school steps, the window ledges, the low concrete fence, and on the lilac bushes by the fence. Sharp, leafless lilac twigs broke through the snow in places, making the bushes look like gigantic porcupines. Every morning, the school janitor swept the school porch and dug a trenchlike path in the snow from the gate to the steps. There was a long patch of ice before the steps, and younger children loved to run up to the patch and glide all the way up to them, screaming with pleasure. The ice patch was also the source of another sort of students' fun, because teachers sometimes slipped and fell there. Some tenth-graders even named the ice patch "the Teachers' Spot."

I happened to witness our elderly chemistry teacher go sprawling on the spot. She spun on the ice in her bulky fur coat, struggling to get to her feet, until one of the ninth-graders came to help her. I saw how other kids stared at her from the porch and through the school windows and laughed. Even the nice ninth-grader who reached out to save her couldn't help but chuckle. In December, eight weeks into my sex education class, the Teachers' Spot had become my main concern as I walked to school. I didn't feel anxious about my lessons anymore. I thought of them as of some dull but not too unpleasant chore as I made small, cautious steps toward the school porch.

My sex instruction wasn't a success, but at least I managed to fill eight forty-five-minute lessons with information. I'd learned how to make a digestible mix from my three contradictory sources: *Sex Education: The Theses, The Nature of Sexuality,* and Aunt Galya's life stories. I usually used *The Theses* as a frame, Aunt Galya's tales for details and examples, and the mammoth *Nature of Sexuality* for emergencies. Whenever I ran out of things to say, I threw in a Latin word or two.

It was hard to steer Aunt Galya in the needed direction. When she didn't feel well, she would only talk about the deficiencies and repulsive habits of her lovers and of men in general. She slumped down on the couch with a bowl of kasha and talked about smelly breath, nasty sounds, and shriveled body parts. She could go on and on, stopping only occasionally to eat a spoonful. Finally, she would usually get up moaning, dump kasha into the garbage, and pour herself some moonshine, looking defeated and guilty. When she felt better, she would sit at the table with a box of candies and talk about her heroic qualities as a lover, laughing heartily and devouring one candy after another. "He was lying there out of breath, all drenched with sweat, and I wasn't even slightly tired! You should've seen the look on his face when I said, 'How about another go?' I thought he'd die right there." Oddly enough, those "better" sessions ended in the same way as the "worse" ones, with a portion of moonshine.

I knew that my students wouldn't be interested in any of that. Techniques and precautions were the information that they needed. And so did I, but it was awfully hard to guide Aunt Galya toward the things I wanted to know. When she yielded, I grabbed my notebook and scribbled down the precious facts to retell them to the girls later.

Yet I was afraid of students' questions. I lay in bed at night imagining what would happen if the girls asked me something. I tossed and turned, sometimes trying to figure out a way to dodge questions, sometimes simply praying that the girls would be too shy to ask me anything.

And they were shy, at first. They sat tense and silent, afraid to show any reaction to what I said. But as the lessons progressed, they relaxed more. They smiled or gasped or exchanged looks, sometimes whispering to each other. And then one day, I saw a terrifying sight—Sveta Zotova raising her hand. I had a feeling she wasn't just going to ask for permission to go to the bathroom. Her beautiful narrow hand with long fingers and manicured fingernails looked like a deadly snake. "Sometimes we want to know something in particular. Can we ask questions?" My stomach dropped. I fingered a piece of gum stuck to my desk and thought, "No! No! You can't!" But Sveta was still talking: "We could ask anonymous questions. Can we write them on pieces of paper and leave them here?" I almost let out a sigh of relief. It was the perfect solution. It would leave me enough time to consult a book or Aunt Galya.

The girls put a brown shoebox under my desk and started leaving their questions in there after Friday math lessons. There were only one or two questions each week, most of them from Sveta Zotova. I recognized her neat, firm handwriting and perfect logic: "I read that oral contraception is 97 percent safe. Does that take into account the times when a person forgets to take the pill? If not, what would be the correct percentage?" Other girls' notes weren't as good, and some were barely legible, with spelling mistakes, omitted words, and words crossed out or written over others. The questions covered everything from contraception to breast enlargement to behavior on a date. One girl (poor Vera Bunina, probably) asked, "What should I do if I am on a date and I really have to pee and I don't want the boy to know that I'm going to the bathroom?" Aunt Galya was annoyed by questions like that. "Let her pee in her pants if she is such an idiot!" I, on the contrary, loved these silly questions more than Sveta's serious ones. I could imagine my girls going out on dates and experiencing these difficulties. I liked to act out these situations in my head, with me as the main character, and think about what I would do. At times, I actually enjoyed my lessons.

ABOUT FOUR WEEKS into my sex lessons, the other teachers had started treating me differently. They never asked me about my lessons, or made any remarks about them, but they actually became aware of my existence. It felt so strange, as if I'd suddenly lost a magic hat that had made me invisible all the time. They still didn't consider me a colleague—I hadn't been admitted to their gossip circle—but they nodded to me when we met in the hall and talked to me about minor events at the school: "Did you hear that a cafeteria window was broken?" They even asked me about my private life: "When are your exams?" (Younger teachers.) Or "Do you miss your mother?" (Older teachers.) I didn't feel that I was in a vacuum anymore.

Sergey started noticing me too. I caught him looking in my direction with a questioning expression, as if he didn't know what to make of me. At times, he'd stop by my room and peek in, but then leave without saying anything. Or he would stare at me and squint his eyes as he did when he wanted to make fun of somebody, but then turn away again without saying anything. I was a perfect target for him. An incompetent sex education teacher! It made me nervous but, at the same time, oddly pleased.

Maria Mikhailovna, on the other hand, began paying less attention to me. After asking me to show her my list of topics and collating it carefully with the one suggested by *Sex Education: The Theses,* she was content to let me teach. She never peeked in during my sex lessons, either because she didn't care what I was saying, or because she didn't want to be responsible if I taught the girls something wrong. I was happy that she also peeked in less frequently during my math lessons, perhaps afraid that I'd start talking about sex.

MY ONLY PROBLEM was that after a while I started doubting Aunt Galya's expertise. At bedtime, I tossed under my thin woolen blanket and wondered: "What if Aunt Galya was wrong? What if lemon juice wasn't good enough as a contraceptive? What if eating a lot of cabbage didn't make your breasts bigger? What if hair on your legs wasn't a sign of infertility? What if Aunt Galya's whole attitude toward men was wrong?" The last question bothered me the most. Aunt Galya seemed to see men as soldiers in an enemy army. Even more than that, as soldiers defeated and captured. "Don't let them sneak away!" "Make them work very hard!" "Don't let them get lazy!" "Don't reward them until they deserve it." Cold sweat broke out on my forehead when I remembered repeating Aunt Galya's words in my lessons. I looked at the portraits of Aunt Galya's late husbands, glistening softly in the moonlight above my head. They didn't look very happy. And they were both dead.

Sometimes during my math lessons I would look at the boys and wonder how much they knew about the girls' sex instruction. I wondered if Sveta shared some of Aunt Galya's wisdom with her boyfriend Sasha Smirnov? A few other girls had boyfriends from the same class too. I was sure the boys knew something now. They avoided looking at me. They sat at their desks trying to be as quiet as possible, trying not to do anything that would attract my attention. They acted as if I knew something bad about them, something that they didn't want me to know. A few times, I had the urge to go back on my words, to say that it wasn't me talking, it was Aunt Galya! And then I would think about Sergey. What if the boys talked to Sergey about my lessons? I imagined Sasha Smirnov raising his hand, lifting his big body out of the desk with a crash—he couldn't move quietly—fingering a jacket button and saying in his deep-voiced monotone, "The girls' teacher said that men . . ." I wondered what Sergey's reaction would be. Every time he looked at me with his new, questioning look, I wondered if he was thinking it was I who hated men.

Sergey finally talked to me during the lunch hour in our school cafeteria. The cafeteria served only preprepared lunches, one or two combinations each day of the week. On

Fridays we could choose sardelki with beet salad or herring with mashed potatoes. I would have preferred sardelki with mashed potato, but you couldn't change a combination. The sardelki, my favorite food, had hard skins and tasted better than the usual franks. I loved how the juice burst into my mouth when I sank my teeth into them. I hated beet salad. Few things could be more appalling than chunks of overcooked beets with potatoes and carrots swimming in a pool of smelly sunflower oil, but I decided to put up with it for the sake of the sardelki.

I sat down at the teachers' table and began piercing my sardelki with a fork when Sergey tapped me on the shoulder. He stood grinning by my chair with a plate of herring and mashed potatoes. "Don't let them sneak away; make them work very hard!" He winked at me and walked to his usual place at the end of table. My heart jumped up and down inside my chest. I spent the rest of the lunch break waiting for Sergey to continue. I chewed hard on the sardelki and shook the excess oil off the cubes of potato and beet. I was sure that Sergey had already thought of what to say; he was only waiting for the opportunity to speak. I had the terrifying thought that he somehow, through some unimaginable source, had become aware of Aunt Galya's existence and he would ask about her. I grew tired of waiting—I almost wished that Sergey would strike sooner. I stole a quick glance in his direction. He wasn't looking at me. He was working on his lunch, pulling bones out of the herring and laying them on the edge of his plate. It was a perfect chance to escape. I left my plate and hurried out of the cafeteria. I almost made it to the exit when I heard Sergey's voice again, rustling somewhere above my ears, the words barely audible amid the cafeteria's steady rumble. I had to lift up my face to make out what he was saying. He was asking me on a date.

THE FOLLOWING MONDAY, I woke up early. I had set the alarm for 8 A.M., but when I opened my eyes, the room was still dark and my fluorescent clock read only 6:30. I had come home from my date with Sergey at about 10 P.M. and had taken off my only skirt and my pantyhose before I collapsed onto my bed and fell asleep.

I stuck the tips of my toes out from under my blanket and immediately pulled them back. The room was frigid. Normally, I would have stayed in bed until the alarm clock rang, all bundled up like a cocoon, but that day I simply couldn't keep still. My limbs felt like they were filled with tight little springs, longing to be released, pushing me to move, stir, do something. I sprang off the bed and attempted to do some aerobics on the little rug by the wardrobe, but my feet kept bumping against the bed. My reflection in the mirrored wardrobe surface—barefoot, wrinkled blouse, tousled hair—seemed awfully funny for some reason. I plopped down on my bed and started laughing, pressing my hands to my mouth so that I wouldn't wake Aunt Galya. I thought of phoning home—my mother usually woke up early. I even took the receiver off the cradle, but then I put it down. I knew that I wouldn't be able to stop laughing, and my mother would think that I was crying, and it would be impossible to prove that I really wasn't. That too seemed awfully funny, and I sat and laughed until I became aware that I was famished.

In the kitchen, I sprinkled a piece of rye bread with salt and ate it standing in the doorway. Aunt Galya was stretched out on her bed in striped men's pajamas, her blanket on the floor. She slept on her back, pressing a small pillow to her chest as if it were a teddy bear. I walked over to her, covered her with the blanket, and tiptoed out of the room.

WHEN I ARRIVED at the school, the streetlamps were still lit, shining yellow rings of light onto the snow, making the snow seem soft and warm. The path to the porch had been freshly swept and the Teachers' Spot glistened. Aside from the school janitor with his fuzzy broom, there wasn't anybody in the schoolyard. If I slipped and fell, nobody would see me. I ran up to the Teachers' Spot, pushed with one foot, and glided to the porch without falling.

In my classroom, I opened a window, letting in an icy, swishing gust of wind. I sat down at my desk, then immediately stood up and walked to Tanya Myshkina's desk in the first row. I couldn't sit there either. I walked to the back of the room and sat in Vera Bunina's chair for a minute, then on the edge of her desk. The thought occurred to me that I was behaving just like Goldilocks, trying out my students' chairs and desks. What if I told the girls about my date with

Sergey? What if I told them what a promising expression he had in his eyes? What if I told them how his hand got stuck in the knot of my scarf when he tried to unbutton my coat in a crowded movie theater? And how later he kissed me through the entire *Godfather: Part III,* pausing only when he perceived, with his peripheral vision, that one or another of the characters was about to be killed. He let me go then and watched him die, while I wished that the death would be quick. What if I told them that the best part of the date wasn't even being on a date, but walking to our meeting place at the Pushkin subway stop, because men turned to look at me when I walked. I wondered if the girls would be able to understand any of it. I imagined how I would talk to them, sitting on the edge of Vera's desk like this, swaying my legs and laughing.

Then I saw something that made the laughing springs go quiet somewhere in the pit of my stomach, replaced by the familiar sensation of panic. The brown shoebox lay under my teacher's desk, looking small and deceptively harmless. I had forgotten to pick up the questions on Friday. I slowly slid off Vera's desk and walked to the box. Inside was a notebook page folded in four. My first thought was to throw it away, to get rid of it, and pretend that there wasn't anything in the box. But what if by some miracle I knew the answer? I unfolded the note. About half of the page was covered with firm, rounded letters. It looked like Sveta Zotova's handwriting, but it wasn't as neat as her usual notes—she must have been nervous when she wrote it. I smoothed the paper in my hands and read the question quickly.

I read it a second time, this time aloud, right after the bell had rung and the girls had taken their places at their desks. "I've been dating Boy X for some months now, I like him very much, we have a steady relationship. When he touches me in certain places, it feels very good. But lately I've gone out with Boy Y a few times. He doesn't read books, he has a dumb laugh and pimples."

I paused and looked out at the class. Some of the girls took quick looks around, trying to guess the author. Others seemed genuinely interested in the problem itself. With their mouths open and their brows pulled together, they strained to digest the question and possibly apply it to themselves. In the first row, Tanya Myshkina was chewing the tip of her pen so hard it seemed she might bite off a piece and swallow it. I tried not to embarrass Sveta by looking at her, but with my peripheral vision I saw that she was gazing out the window at the concrete schoolyard, twisting and twisting her curls on her finger. I cleared my throat and read the note to the end. "I don't like Boy Y at all. Why then, when he touches me in certain places, do I feel exactly the same as with Boy X?" Now they were all looking at me. They seriously thought that I could answer the question.

The ticklish springs of laughter were coming back, building up somewhere in my chest and struggling to get higher and higher. And then I said something that I'd been wanting to say for a very long time.

"I don't know!"

I enjoyed saying these words so much that it made me light-headed. I felt like hopping on one foot around the classroom singing, "I don't know! I don't know! I don't know!" The springs of laughter were growing bigger and bigger, breaking through my skin, leaving my body, filling the room. Then I heard the first sounds of giggling. I wasn't sure if it was me or one of the girls. Soon everybody was laughing, even Sveta Zotova. Soon the separate sounds became simply one loud, steady rumble in the room. I didn't hear Maria Mikhailovna open the classroom door. I couldn't hear what she was saying. I only saw the tips of her black shoes, and her pink face squeezed between the door and the doorframe, her eyelashes blinking and her lips moving. If she was saying anything about inappropriate behavior and disrespect to the young teacher, none of us could hear it.

About the Author

Lara Vapnyar emigrated from Russia to New York in 1994, and began publishing short stories in English in 2002. Her work has appeared in *Open City* and *The New Yorker.* She lives on Staten Island and is pursuing a Ph.D. in comparative literature at The Graduate Center of the City University of New York.

A Note on the Type

This book was set in Minion, a typeface produced by the Adobe Corporation specifically for the Macintosh personal computer, and released in 1990. Designed by Robert Slimbach, Minion combines the classic characteristics of old style faces with the full compliment of weights required for modern typesetting.

Composed by Stratford Publishing, Brattleboro, Vermont

Printed and bound by R. R. Donnelley,

Harrisonburg, Virginia